When it comes to vampires and cowboys...
nobody does it better than Kimberly Raye!

"Kimberly Raye is a wonderful writer whose powerful imagination creates such appealing and realistic characters that will draw readers and captivate them."
—*A Romance Review* on *Dead End Dating*

"Kimberly Raye has done a wonderful job of creating characters that are unique and imaginative!"
—*Romance Reviews Today* on *Dead and Dateless*

"Humor, witty dialogue, a good setup and a great hero and heroine make Raye's book sparkle."
—*Romantic Times BOOKreviews* on *Texas Fire*

"Amusing, erotic... A very naughty book!
You'll love it."
—*Romantic Reviews* on *Sometimes Naughty,
Sometimes Nice*

"Kimberly Raye pens a delightfully sexy and funny tale with wonderful characterization, warm dialogue and humorous scenes."
—*Romantic Times BOOKreviews*

"Ms. Raye's creative plotting and vivid characterizations herald a strong new voice in romantic fiction."
—*Romantic Times BOOKreviews*

Blaze™

Dear Reader,

Welcome back to Skull Creek, Texas! Where the women are smart and sexy and the men are...*vampires*?

Yep, that's right. We're talking bloodsucker with a capital *B*.

Of course, Dillon Cash, the hero in my newest Harlequin Blaze novel, *Drop Dead Goregous*, isn't just any old vamp. Dillon, once the geekiest guy in town, is reveling in his newfound vamp charisma. His mission as the new undead stud extraordinaire? To break the town's standing record for sleeping with the most women. A piece of cake when every female within a fifty-mile radius now finds him irresistible.

Every female, that is, except Meg Sweeney. Meg, his old high school friend, isn't the least bit anxious to hop into bed with him. No, she's more anxious to learn the secret to his sudden sex appeal. Meg—who was once a card-carrying member of the Geek Squad herself—is ready to sex up her own image and Dillon's just the cowboy to help her. Or so she thinks...

I hope you enjoy this next installment in my Texas vampire series. I would love to hear from you! You can visit me online at www.kimberlyraye.com or write to me c/o Harlequin Books, 225 Duncan Mill Road, Don Mills, Ontario M3B 3K9, Canada.

Enjoy, and y'all come back now, ya hear!

Kimberly Raye

KIMBERLY RAYE
Drop Dead
Gorgeous

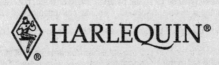

HARLEQUIN®

TORONTO • NEW YORK • LONDON
AMSTERDAM • PARIS • SYDNEY • HAMBURG
STOCKHOLM • ATHENS • TOKYO • MILAN • MADRID
PRAGUE • WARSAW • BUDAPEST • AUCKLAND

ISBN-13: 978-0-373-79394-5
ISBN-10:   0-373-79394-4

DROP DEAD GORGEOUS

www.eHarlequin.com

Printed in U.S.A.

ABOUT THE AUTHOR

USA TODAY bestselling author Kimberly Raye has always been an incurable romantic. While she enjoys reading all types of fiction, her favorites, the books that touch her soul, are romance novels. From sexy to thrilling, sweet to humorous, she likes them all. But what she really loves is writing romance—the hotter the better! She started her first novel in high school and has been writing ever since. Kim lives deep in the heart of the Texas Hill Country with her very own cowboy, Curt, and their young children. She talks regularly with her therapist (aka her editor) and spends most of her time cooking up new story ideas. She's also an avid reader (she reads *all* the Blaze books) who loves Diet Dr. Pepper, chocolate, Toby Keith, chocolate, alpha males—*especially* vampires—and chocolate. Kim loves to hear from readers. You can visit her online at www.kimberlyraye.com or at www.myspace.com/kimberlyrayebooks.

Books by Kimberly Raye
HARLEQUIN BLAZE

For my caring, supportive, ultra-fabulous editor
Brenda Chin, for NOT moving to England.

1

IT WAS THE BEST SEX she'd had in months.

The only sex.

Which wouldn't have been such a bad thing except that the elusive O came courtesy of a red fluorescent vibrator called the Big Tamale rather than some hot, buff cowboy with a slow hand and an intoxicating smile.

Margaret Evelyn Sweeney, aka Meg, hit the three different Off buttons—vibrate, swivel and *aye carumba*—and stashed Big in its matching red case. She drew a deep breath, swung her legs over the side of her bed and got to her feet.

Five minutes later, she stood in her kitchen and leaned over a hot-pink three-ring binder—her own personal Pleasure Manual—to document tonight's results. She flipped to page fifty-eight, which included a quick summation of last Tuesday's class entitled *Masturbation Mania* and a worksheet for homework. She scribbled in the date and tackled the questions.

Intense sensation? Check.

Spontaneous groaning (the good kind)? Check.

Uncontrollable moaning? Check.

A full-blown scream? Check.

Overall level of satisfaction?

She eyed the scale that ranged from one to ten, *zip* to *zowee*, and finally circled *seven* before moving on to the last question.

Did this sexual experience include a partner? She ignored the crazy urge to jot down a big fat *yes*. This wasn't about soothing her fragile ego and saving face with the other women in the painfully small town of Skull Creek, Texas.

The whole purpose of attending carnal classes with a certified carnal coach was to invest in her future. Sadly enough, she was thirty years old and she could count on one hand the number of romantic entanglements she'd had in her lifetime.

Actually, she could count them on two fingers. Three if she included her encounters with her good buddy and childhood friend, Dillon Cash. While Meg had been a mega tomboy, Dillon had been a major geek. Either way, they'd both never really fit in with the opposite sex—not romantically—and so they'd turned to each other back in the ninth grade when they'd realized that they were the only ones—with the exception of Connie Louise Davenport, Reverend Davenport's daughter—in the entire freshman class who hadn't known how to French kiss.

Okay, so they hadn't known how to kiss, period. No quick pecks. No slow, lingering smooches. No open mouths and plunging tongues. They'd been fifteen and very green, and so it had seemed like a good idea to work out the awkwardness with each other.

Several hours, a bootleg copy of a *Nine 1/2 Weeks* video, and a dozen clumsy attempts later, they hadn't been any more skilled than when they'd started.

In fact, the entire experience had solidified what she'd known from the get-go—Dillon was and would always be just a good friend. She hadn't liked him like *that*.

No heart stutters. No tummy tingles. No rip-off-your-panties-and-go-bonkers lust.

Which was why, despite the experimental kissing, she felt inclined to leave him out of the tally when it came to her sexual past.

That left Oren and Walter. She'd lost her virginity to Oren, aka the Orenator, at the ripe old age of eighteen. He'd been the best defensive end the Skull Creek Panthers had ever seen, and he'd taken them to the state championship during his senior year. *And* he'd actually liked her, enough to ask her out for Homecoming.

They'd gone to the school dance, and then they'd gone parking down by the river.

Ten minutes in the backseat of his daddy's Chevy listening to recaps of the Cowboys vs. Redskins game, and she'd had enough. She'd thrown her arms around him, pressed her body up against his and offered herself shamelessly. Other than a few initial moments of shock and a frantic "What are you doing?", he'd finally given in to her persistent lips. She'd lost her innocence along with one of her new hoop earrings and her undies.

Yes!

Not that the experience itself had been all that great. While he'd given in, he hadn't taken the initiative and swept her off her feet. Rather, she'd taken the lead, pushing and urging and giving a whole new meaning to her nickname Manhandler Meg.

Still, it had been the principle of the thing. It had been the beginning of a new chapter in her life. A chance to start over. To completely forget the tomboy she'd once been and embrace all that was feminine.

Change.

That's what it had all been about. Meg had grown up being a carbon copy of her father. He'd been a single parent—her mother, a diabetic, had died of renal failure shortly after Meg's birth—and an athletics coach at the local high school. Growing up, Meg had been determined to follow in his footsteps. She'd watched him, learned from him, idolized him, and then one day he'd been gone.

She'd been barely seventeen and it had been the start of the summer after her junior year. She'd gone home early to pack (they were going camping to celebrate the end of classes) and he'd stayed late to finish cleaning out his desk. He'd been in a hurry to get home, not wanting to lose their camping spot at a local state park. He'd failed to stop at a nearby intersection and had been hit by an approaching car. That had been the end of him.

And the end of Meg.

The old Meg.

She'd gone to live with her grandparents and, much to their

surprise, had packed away her soccer ball and kneepads. She'd ditched her favorite baseball bat and glove, her autographed Troy Aikman football and her lucky San Antonio Spurs basketball jersey. Even more, she'd packed away her all-time favorite sweats and the lucky Dallas Cowboy T-shirt her dad had bought her. She'd taken out a subscription to *Cosmo* and had learned all the latest fashion trends. She'd even forfeited helping her granddad on his tractor so that her grandmother could teach her how to sew.

In one summer, she'd traded in her love of sports for an infatuation with shoes and clothes and all things feminine, and had started her senior year as a different Meg. A woman determined to forget her past, to bury it right along with her father.

When Oren had chronicled their night on the wall of the boys' locker room, her undies hanging from one of the locker pegs as proof, she'd been thrilled. The male population of Skull Creek High would finally see her as more than just a competitive edge during game time. She'd been so good at sports that she'd become the best buddy of every male athlete in school. They'd asked her advice on everything from touchdowns to golf putts.

They'd never, however, asked her out.

She'd been convinced that that one wild night with Oren would be enough to change her image.

She'd been wrong.

This was Skull Creek. The classic small town where people left their doors unlocked and the sidewalks rolled up at six o'clock every evening. Forget crime. The most exciting news centered around the occasional boob job or cheating spouse. Strangers were scarce and everyone knew everyone.

And that meant that once she was Manhandler Meg, she'd always be Manhandler Meg.

While she'd managed to change who she actually was, she'd never been able to change everyone's perception of her.

Not way back when Oren had written about her and the entire football team had assumed it was a really great practical joke— she'd gotten so many high fives that her hand had been raw—and not now that she wore high heels and sexy clothes and ran her own dress boutique, It's All About You, a small, exclusive shop located on Main Street, smack dab between Dillon's computer repair shop and the town's one and only full-service spa, Pam's Pamper Park.

People still saw her as a chip-off-the-old-Sweeney-block. The women rarely felt threatened and the men…Well, they actually *respected* her.

While she knew that most females would kill to be valued for their minds rather than their bodies, once, just *once,* she would like to have a man actually see her as a sex object.

So make a real change, pack your bags and get out of Dodge.

She'd thought about it. But the notion of leaving her grandparents—even though they now lived an hour away in a retirement community outside of Austin, and she only saw them a few times a month—was even less appealing than being known as Manhandler Meg for the rest of her life. They'd helped her through her father's death, loved her, raised her, and she intended to return the favor. They'd been there for her when she'd needed them the most, and she intended to be there for them when the time came and they eventually needed her. She couldn't do that if she was God knows where.

Which meant she was here and she was staying.

Walter had been her second romantic entanglement. One that had continued over the years, on during football season and off after the Super Bowl, which kicked off the start of tax season— he was an accountant. While she knew Walter found her attractive, he also liked to pick her brain for betting advice (he spear-headed the weekly football pool at his office). When he won, he got *very* happy and the sex was pretty good—*if* she initiated (Walter wasn't one for making the first move). When he wasn't making money betting on his favorite sport, he was so boring he made a wedge of cheese look exciting.

He was neck-deep in IRS forms and for the past three months, she'd been flying solo.

A good thing, she reminded herself. Walter wasn't the man for her and so she'd broken things off for good after the last Super Bowl. She didn't want a man who only wanted her some of the time. Even more, she didn't want a man who didn't want her enough to make the first move. She was through initiating sex.

Hence the classes.

They'd originally been given by Dillon's sister, Cheryl Anne, who'd been desperate to break out of her shell and do something wild and crazy with her own life. She'd succeeded for a few weeks before she'd realized that actually having sex was much more preferable than talking about it with a bunch of clueless women eager to spice up their relationships. She'd handed over her classes to Winona, the owner of the only motel in town, and had married her long-time boyfriend. Cheryl Anne was now living the American dream.

Not that Meg's goal was to get married. Maybe. Someday. If the right man came along. Right now, however, she simply wanted to have sex with a man who really and truly wanted to have sex with her. A man who couldn't keep his hands off her.

A man who wanted her badly enough to make the first move.

The classes would teach her how to increase her sex appeal to the point that she was irresistible. Hopefully.

Meg finished documenting her results, closed her Pleasure Manual and headed back upstairs to her bedroom closet. After careful consideration, she settled for a hot-pink shell, a frayed blue jean miniskirt with rhinestone trim and a pair of high-heeled sandals she'd picked up on her latest shopping trip to Austin. The outfit met all of her must-haves—feminine and sexy and uber-trendy—which was why it had made it into her closet in the first place. As owner of the one and only upscale boutique in town, she wanted her own personal wardrobe to reflect her business image. While she might be striking out when it came to changing everyone's perception of her personally, professionally she was batting one thousand.

Her shop had become the go-to place for every special

occasion—from proms to anniversary parties to the occasional hot date. Women sought her advice on clothes, shoes and accessories, and her shop had even been named *Business of the Year* three consecutive times in a row by the Skull Creek Chamber of Commerce.

But while her shop was making the news, Meg wasn't.

Meaning she'd yet to garner even a mention in Tilly Townsend's infamous Hot Chicks list. The list was published every six months and featured the ten hottest bachelorettes in town. Likewise, Tilly also did a Randiest Rooster list that named the ten hottest bachelors. The list was the ultimate when it came to popularity—a who's who of the most sought-after singles in town. The women were smart, successful, vivacious and irresistible to men. The newest version came out in exactly two weeks and Meg wanted to be on it.

Meg ignored an inkling of hopelessness and headed for the shower.

She spent the next half hour upstairs getting ready and the last fifteen minutes downstairs sucking down a Diet Coke and re-reading her notes on last week's lesson. She was seated at her table, about to get to the *Understanding Your Vibrator* section, when a tongue lapped at her bare thigh.

She glanced down at the black-and-gray Blue Heeler who'd pushed through the doggy door and now stood next to her. Tail wagging, tongue lolling, the animal stared up at her, a pleading look in her big brown eyes.

"Don't even think it." She wagged a finger at her. "You know what the vet said. Sugar isn't good for a dog your age." Babe, named for the infamous Babe Ruth, obviously disagreed. She wagged her way over to the pantry and stared hopefully at the closed door.

"You can't have any," Meg told the dog, pushing to her feet. She bypassed the pantry to retrieve a small box from a nearby cabinet. "Doc said you could have a veggie biscuit instead." She held out the foul-smelling treat. Babe approached, took one sniff and wagged her way back over to the pantry. She nuzzled the door.

"No," Meg said, but the dog kept pleading.

Five minutes and some serious whimpering later, Meg pulled out a box of golden cakes and fed one to the anxious dog. Babe was getting old. Sixteen to be exact, which meant she no longer had the energy to chase Frisbees or bark at Mrs. Calico's Chihuahua next door. She'd given up chasing balls, too, and carting in the newspaper. Other than watching re-runs of *Sex and the City* and eating the occasional Twinkie, she had zero pleasure in her old age.

Meg fed her a second and smiled as she wolfed it down.

The dog whimpered for a third, but Meg shook her head. "Discipline, girl. It's all about discipline." She stuffed the box back into the pantry and closed the door.

Babe licked at Meg's fingers for a few seconds before heading back to the den and her doggy bed, obviously satisfied for the moment.

If only Meg felt the same.

Despite the orgasm, she was still restless. Anxious. Unfulfilled.

Because she was still every bit as invisible as she'd been way back when. That's why she was taking carnal classes. She wanted men to notice her, to lust after her, to find her completely irresistible.

The way the women were now lusting after Dillon Cash.

She stared at the lifestyle section of the *Skull Creek Gazette* spread out on her kitchen table and her gaze snagged on Tilly's weekly column—What's Hot and What's Not.

A picture of Dillon taken at Joe Bob's Bar & Grill blazed back at her. He was boot scootin' his way across the sawdust floor with Amelia Louise Lauderfield. The infamous Amelia Louise Lauderfield. Number six on Tilly's Hot Chicks list.

Dillon and a bona fide Hot Chick.

Meg still couldn't believe it.

One minute he'd been spending his Saturday nights holed up in his computer repair shop, and the next—a few months ago to be exact—he'd shown up in a nearby town at a local honky tonk, of all places. He'd ditched his glasses and swapped his button-down shirt and slacks for well-worn jeans and a T-shirt. Even more, he'd traded his car, complete with seat belts and air bags, for a custom-made motorcycle and no helmet.

It hadn't been the news of his physical transformation that had startled her so much as everyone's response to it—every female in the Cherry Blossom Saloon had fallen all over themselves for a chance to go home with him.

Then again, word had it he'd shown up after happy hour, which meant that the liquor had been flowing. More than likely, the members of his instant fan club had been extremely drunk. On top of that, the place was out of town. The women who'd gone gaga over his new look couldn't have been privy to his reputation.

At least that's the conclusion she'd come to after one of her customers, Cornelia Wallace, had relayed the rumors circulating around town. She could still hear the old woman's words.

"He's having one of them middle-aged life crisis things. I saw a special about it on the Discovery Health Channel. Said the threat of aging makes a man do crazy things."

"Don't you have to be middle-aged to have a midlife crisis?" Meg had asked the old woman. "Dillon's only thirty."

"Maybe it's one of them there near-death experiences. They did a *20/20* special about them last week. Said folks do all sorts of bizarre things when they almost meet their maker. Or maybe he's having a coming-out-of-the-closet moment and he's fighting it by trying to prove his manhood. Saw just such a thing on one of them cable channels last month. It was all about how this fella actually slept with three dozen women and fathered twenty-two young 'uns just so's he could prove to himself that he wasn't buttering his bread on the wrong side. What do you think?"

"I think you spend too much time watching television. Maybe it wasn't even Dillon over at the saloon. Maybe it was just someone who looked like him."

"It was him, all right. Heard it straight from Evangeline

Dupree, who heard it from her granddaughter, who heard it from her boyfriend who was there having his bachelor party. He swore it was Dillon."

But Meg wasn't so sure. Dillon at a saloon? Getting comfy with a bunch of women?

Not the Dillon she knew.

While they didn't spend a lot of time together now—he was busy at his shop and she was busy with her customers, so they only managed the occasional lunch—she still saw enough of him to know that he was every bit as awkward around the opposite sex as he'd been back in high school.

Up until two months ago, that is.

That's when things had changed.

When *he'd* changed.

Not that she'd seen the transformation firsthand. No, he'd been avoiding her, canceling their lunches, dodging her phone calls. She'd stopped by his shop to see him and put an end to all the nonsense that was flying around—there had to be a logical explanation, right?—but the place had been locked up tight. Ditto for his house. She'd even called his parents, but they'd been as confused as she was, and even more determined to hunt him down and find out the truth.

They'd been camping out in his yard for the past two weeks, trying to corner him and save him from himself.

Meg wasn't one-hundred-percent convinced that the sex object running around town was really him and so she'd taken a less radical approach—she'd left tons of messages on his cell. But he hadn't called her back.

Because he really was busy with his new social life?

Or because he'd left town for yet another computer seminar?

Everyone had a twin somewhere. More than likely Dillon's had moved to the next town and his midlife crisis/near-death-experience/coming-out-of-the-closet was simply a case of mistaken identity. One which he couldn't disprove because he was off learning how to tweak motherboards or dissect USB switches or something.

And the picture staring back at her?

Dillon's twin.

Maybe. Probably.

Sure, it would be great if he really *had* managed such a change. Then he could give her some pointers on how to nail *irresistible* and make it onto Tilly's Hot Chicks list. But Meg wasn't getting her hopes up. She knew the hazards of living in a small town. Last year Diana Trucker had been spotted buying a pregnancy test at the local pharmacy. By the time Meg had heard the news from Corny, the woman had been six months pregnant with quintuplets.

People had a way of exaggerating everything.

Which meant, until she saw actual proof of Dillon's newfound sex appeal, she wasn't buying one word of Corny's gossip.

She had her own sex appeal—or lack of—to worry over.

She'd just finished an online *How to Sex Up Your Image* seminar in addition to several self-help classes at the local junior college—*Dressing for Sexcess* and *How to Lick Your Lips Like You Mean It*. If that wasn't enough, she was now taking carnal Classes being offered in the lobby of the Skull Creek Inn.

At least that's what she told herself as she showered and dressed. She didn't want to be late for tonight's class.

SHE HAD TO BE SEEING things.

Meg sat in the motel parking lot near the corner of the building and stared across the dimly lit walkway that ran the length of the first floor. She stared through the windshield of her Mustang and her gaze zeroed in on the profile of the man who stood in front of the doorway to room four.

He wore snug, faded jeans, a fitted black T-shirt and a pair of black cowboy boots. A black Resistol tipped low on his forehead and cast a shadow across the top half of his face. Dark blond hair curled from beneath the hat brim and brushed the collar of his shirt. He was tall and muscular and...*Dillon*.

She blinked, but he didn't disappear. And neither did the beautiful woman pressed up against his back, her arms locked around his waist as she waited for him to slide the key into the lock and open the door.

A heartbeat later, the door opened and he pried the woman loose long enough to step aside and motion her into the room. She slid by him, her hands brushing his crotch before she disappeared inside.

He quickly followed and Meg was left to wonder if Corny had been right and she'd just witnessed the transformation of a lifetime. That couldn't have been Dillon Cash.

Yes. No. *Hell*, no.

The next few minutes were spent debating between the three as she gathered up her purse and Pleasure Manual, climbed from the front seat and headed for the hotel lobby.

She didn't mean to slow down, but she couldn't help herself. She paused briefly at the door to room four, but the only sound she heard was the frantic beating of her own heart.

2

"LET'S DO IT RIGHT NOW," the soft, breathless voice slid into his ears and sent a burst of *yeah, right* straight to his brain. *"Please."*

Dillon Cash stared at the woman who'd preceded him into the motel room, her eyes gleaming with a mix of passion and desperation. He barely resisted the urge to pinch himself.

No way was this happening.

This was Susie Wilcox, a former Homecoming Queen and now the hottest divorcée in Skull Creek, according to the local paper and Tilly Townsend who'd given the sexy blonde the number one spot on last year's Hot Chicks list.

Rumor had it Susie was a shoo-in for this year's list, as well.

She had long, silky hair. Legs up to *here*. Breasts out to *there*. Her tiny waist begged for his hands and her heart-shaped ass made his mouth go dry. She'd been the star of his wettest dreams back in high school, and a few dozen erotic fantasies in the twelve-plus years since.

She was everything he'd ever wanted in a woman and she was here.

Now.

With *him*.

And she was getting naked.

She kicked off her high heels, grabbed the edge of her tank top and pulled the cotton up and over her head. Popping the buttons on her jeans, she shimmied the ultra-tight denim down her long legs and stepped free. Her fingers went to her bra clasp and just like that, her impressive DD's popped free. She stood before him then wearing a pink mesh thong that left little to the imagination and a rosy red flush that said she was as hot and bothered as a woman could get.

Surprise snaked through him, but he tamped it back down and focused on the hunger stirring deep inside of him.

"I can't stop thinking about you," she said. Her gaze, intense and unwavering, glittered with passion. "About us." She shook her head. "I don't know why, but the first moment I saw you tonight, I knew we would end up here." She smiled. "I feel like I can't keep my hands off of you." The smile faded into a look of raw, inexplicable need. "I feel like I'm going to explode right now if I don't get close to you." She moved toward him, eating up the distance between them with determined steps. "*Very* close."

Maybe she wasn't privy as to *why* she wanted him so badly. And Dillon wasn't about to tell her.

It had started two months ago when a stranger had ridden into town. Jake McCann had turned out to be more than the average drifter. He'd been a vampire determined to lay his past to rest, to slay his demons. Literally. And Dillon had gotten caught in the middle of the struggle.

One minute Dillon had been trying to protect an old friend and the next, he'd had a pair of bloodthirsty fangs—courtesy of Jake's nemesis—gnawing at his neck. He'd come *this close* to dying, his life spilling away on the pavement of the town's main square, but then Jake had stepped forward, shared his own blood, and changed Dillon forever.

Thankfully.

Sure, it wasn't the most practical lifestyle—no more lounging on the beach or scarfing chicken fried steak. But being bitten and turned into a vampire who thrived on blood *and* sex—especially sex—wasn't such a bad thing.

Not to a man whose parents had been a pair of obsessive-compulsives who'd worried about *everything*, particularly the health and well-being of their only two children. Dillon and his younger sister, Cheryl Anne, had been smothered and coddled to the point that they'd been isolated from their peers. Harold and Dora Cash had never taken their children on a trip to the beach—and risk the possibility of sun damage? Nor had they allowed them to eat chicken fried steak or anything with an overabundance of trans fat.

Dillon had grown up playing solitaire and chess while other kids went camping and joined Boy Scouts. He'd also been a computer whiz who'd spent his summers reading and taking online courses instead of catching fireflies and going on picnics or swimming down at Skull Creek river.

At thirty-one, he'd become his own boss—he owned the only computer store within a fifty mile radius that handled both new sales and repairs. He was independent, financially solvent, and still a major geek.

Up until two months ago, that is.

"Once a geek, always a geek."

Susie's words echoed in his head. That's what she'd told him back in high school when he'd worked up the nerve to ask her out. He'd gotten a new haircut and ordered a cool pair of jeans and an AC/DC T-shirt online. He'd even invested the money he'd made typing English papers on a pair of contact lenses. But it hadn't been enough. By then, the damage had already been done, his reputation established. His new look had failed. Even more, one of his contacts had popped out and Susie had ground it into the concrete as she'd spun on her heel, told him to get lost and walked away.

Her rejection had set the stage for many more to come. He'd gone on to have a measly three sexual encounters in his lifetime (not counting the experimental petting he'd done with his buddy Meg back in the ninth grade), and not one woman had ever come back for seconds.

In fact, he'd had a pretty hard time talking them into firsts.

All that had changed the night he'd been turned.

He'd changed.

A gleam of yellow pushed through the part in the drapes and sliced across the carpet at his feet, but it did little to illuminate the rest of the room. He blinked, his gaze piercing the darkness, drinking in every detail of the small hotel room—from the faint scars on the worn dresser to the tiny thread that unraveled at the corner of the bedspread, to the shimmering spiderweb that dangled in the far corner. His vision had improved and sharpened to the point that he had no need of the black coke-bottle glasses he'd worn since the age of five.

His dark blond hair was shinier and thicker, too, his body more muscular and defined. His acne had completely cleared up and his tongue no longer tied itself into knots when a pretty female looked his way.

Now he knew exactly how to talk to a woman.

How to look at her. To touch. To seduce.

He was now a vampire who craved sexual energy as much as he craved the sustenance of blood. More, in fact. And after thirty-one years of near celibacy, Dillon Cash had no qualms feeding the hunger that now lived and breathed inside of him.

His nostrils flared and the scent of warm, ripe woman filled his head. His body responded instantly. His hands itched to reach out. His muscles tightened in anticipation. The blood pounded through his veins. His dick stirred, growing hard, hot, *ready*.

Still. As great as he knew the sex would be, this encounter would just make him that much more anxious for the next.

Another woman.

Another rush of succulent, sweet, drenching energy.

He needed it. He thrived on it. He fed off of it.

Gladly.

Unlike the vampire who'd turned him, Dillon wasn't the least bit anxious to escape the hunger. Not when it came with so many perks. He knew he would inevitably miss his humanity. He would then get as serious as Jake about finding and destroying the Ancient One, and putting an end to the vampire curse once and for all.

After he'd broken Bobby McGuire's record for having slept with the most women in town.

Bobby was a legend in Skull Creek. He'd held the number one

spot on the town's Randiest Rooster list for a record twenty-eight years, right up until he'd turned forty-eight and had had his first heart attack. The doc had put him on a strict No Excitement diet, and he'd been booted off the list. Before however, he'd been a major gigolo rumored to have done the deed with over three hundred women, a count he'd recorded by carving notches into his pine headboard. That proof had sold for over two thousand dollars last year at a local charity auction when Bobby, now an old man, had donated a houseful of furniture and moved to a retirement community in Port Aransas.

Over the years, some had called Bobby a sex maniac. Others had called him a liar. A few had even said he was delusional.

But no one—not a single soul—had ever called him a geek.

Not that Dillon cared what other people thought. Nor did he have any desire to land himself on the notorious list.

This wasn't about proving something to the folks of Skull Creek. It was about proving something to himself. After so many years of having zero luck with the opposite sex, he'd started to think that maybe, just maybe, Susie had been right about him.

He'd never really thought so. He'd always walked the straight and narrow because of his parents. He didn't want to cause them any more grief. He'd caused enough as a child when he'd nearly gotten himself killed.

It had been his seventh birthday and he'd been determined to camp out down by the creek. His parents had said no, but he'd snuck out anyway. He'd been walking around without shoes near the water and had stepped on something sharp. In a matter of days, a small puncture wound had morphed into a full-blown staph infection.

A near fatal infection that had turned his parents from normal and easygoing people to smothering and obsessive caretakers in less than six months.

Cheryl Anne was too young to remember—she'd been four at the time—and too young to blame him for the stifled life she'd been forced to lead. But he remembered how things had been before the incident. His parents had been fun-loving and adventurous back then. And Dillon? He'd been outgoing. A risk taker with a zest for life.

He'd buckled under the guilt, suppressed that lust and obeyed his folks from then on. To everyone else, he'd seemed like a quiet, shy, timid kid, but deep inside he'd been just the opposite.

An act. That's all it had been, or so he'd always thought up until he'd graduated high school without even making it to second base with a girl. The doubts had set in then—the notion that maybe he wasn't really pretending. Maybe he really had morphed into a bona fide geek.

Even now that he was a vampire there were still moments—quick bursts of thought whenever he found himself in the most unreal situations—when he knew, he just *knew,* he had to be dreaming and it was just a matter of time before reality intruded and he morphed back to his old, boring self.

But he was going to change all of that and silence the doubts for good. He'd fantasized about breaking Bobby's record—what hormone-driven teenage boy hadn't?—but he'd never had the opportunity.

Until now.

Two months, an uncontrollable hunger and a nearly impossible number of women—he was now only two shy of his goal.

Training his gaze on the tall, voluptuous blonde, he sent a rush of mental images, leaving no doubt in her mind what he wanted to do to her.

She didn't walk away this time. She couldn't. She wanted him with a greedy desperation that she'd never felt for any other man.

He read that truth in her eyes—another vampire perk—along with the fact that, despite her beauty and the prestige of being number one on Tilly's Hottest Chicks list, she was the loneliest and most miserable of all her friends. Contrary to rumor, she hadn't left her second husband because he'd filed bankruptcy after some bad business investments. He'd been cheating on her with a giggling twenty-one-year-old barmaid and had spent their entire savings on hair plugs, liposuction and a penis enlargement.

"Touch me," she begged. "Please."

And because Dillon needed her as much as she needed him, he did.

"CAN ANYONE TELL ME THE key ingredient to a successful relationship?"

Meg wiggled in her seat, craned her neck and peered between two gigantic teased and sprayed hairdos. Her gaze went to the woman who stood center stage in the small lobby of the Skull Creek Inn.

Winona Atkins was well into her seventies. She wore a flower-print smock, white orthopedic shoes and a penis-shaped name tag that read Carnal Coach. Rolls of snow white curls covered her head and a pair of gold-rimmed cat's eye glasses hung from a chain around her neck.

The old woman arched a white eyebrow as she eyed her roomful of eager students. "Well, come on now." She waved a bony hand. "I ain't got all night. Somebody bite the bullet and take a stab at it."

"Honesty?" someone called out.

"Mutual respect?" asked another.

"Separate bank accounts?"

Winona smiled, her face breaking into a mass of wrinkles. "Those are some fine answers, ladies. Mighty fine." She shook her head. "But I'm afraid they ain't even close. See—" she retrieved the hat rack standing in the far corner and hauled it front and center "—every man, no matter how upstanding or uptight he might be, likes a little hooch ever once in a while."

"Hooch?" one woman asked. "Is that like a floozy?"

"Exactly. It's a woman who can cut loose and shed her inhibitions. A woman who's got confidence and isn't afraid to show it. A woman who'll strip buck naked and wrap herself around the nearest pole." Winona gripped the hat rack and did a little shake and shimmy. "I call this move "Circling the wagons", ladies." She went around the cedar rack once, twice. "I know it looks complicated now, but after tonight's lesson, you'll all be able to do it with your eyes closed. Which is a plus if you're like Sally, there, who's got cataracts." She indicated a seventy-something woman straining to see with her bifocals. "Not that you're s'posed to close your eyes. Eye contact is a powerful thing between a woman and a man."

Winona's words stirred a sudden vision of Dillon standing in the hotel doorway, his gaze hooked on Susie Wilcox, his eyes bright. Gleaming. Powerful.

A pang of envy shot through her. A crazy reaction because no way—repeat, no way—was she even remotely attracted to Dillon Cash.

Sure, she'd felt a few tummy tingles when they'd tried the kissing thing way back when, but what red-blooded, curious, hormonal teen girl wouldn't after watching Mickey Rourke seduce Kim Bassinger? It hadn't been Dillon. It had been the heat of the moment.

Luckily, the temperature had quickly fizzled after the first disappointing attempt at a kiss. She hadn't felt even an inkling of attraction to him since.

Not then and certainly not now.

Forget jealous. She was envious. He had a hot woman falling all over him, and she wanted the same. Not a hot woman, mind you, but a hot man.

Yep, she was envious. *If* it was really and truly him, that is.

She latched onto the doubts and turned her attention back to the front of the room.

"…start with Mary." Winona pointed to a woman seated on the front row. "I want you to get up and try circling the wagons. We'll keep going seat by seat until everyone gets a turn. While everyone's trying out the technique, I'll have a look at the homework assignment from the last class."

Pages fluttered as everyone pulled out their notebooks.

"I don't know if I can do this," Mary said as she pushed to her feet. "I'm not used to working with an audience."

"That's what these are for, dear." Winona retrieved a platter of petit fours from a nearby table. "I call 'em pleasure bites. These little buggers will have you stripping off your clothes and shedding your inhibitions quicker than Arlen Wilson can chow through an apple with those new titanium dentures of his."

"Are those made with that wacky tobacky Mildred Pierce always puts in her brownies?" Mary asked.

Winona frowned. "I run a reputable business here, ladies. This here's made with Everclear," Winona said. "Colorless, tasteless and completely legal."

"Well, then." Mary grabbed one and popped it into her mouth before helping herself to a second and then a third. She drew a deep breath and eyed the hat rack.

Meanwhile, Winona handed the platter to the next woman in line and the goodies started to circulate.

"Billy and I had such a good time last night," Mabel Avery told Winona as the old woman stepped toward her and confiscated her journal. "He loved watching me with that pink vibrator I ordered off the Internet."

"My Hank liked watching me, too," another woman said, waving her spiral notebook. "But mine's purple instead of pink."

"My Melvin said it was his fantasy come true," said another.

As the comments continued, Meg made a show of searching around her seat before throwing up her hands. "What do you know? I think I left my notebook in the car," she said to the woman next to her. She pushed to her feet. "I'll just pop out and get it."

Five seconds later, she closed the lobby door behind her and breathed a sigh of relief.

Coward, a voice whispered. *The entire town knows you're unattached.*

But knowing it and hearing it, complete with written documentation to back it up, was a totally different thing. It was bad enough she'd had to try out the vibrator alone. She wasn't going to admit it to a roomful of nosy women.

No, she'd take her time going to the car, then slip back inside once Winona went back to her pole dancing techniques.

She was halfway down the walkway when her gaze snagged on the door to room four.

It was shut solid. The curtains were drawn on the window just to the left. No light spilled past the two-inch gap in the drapes.

Make that a three inch gap.

Not that she was looking.

She was *not* going to look.

That's what she told herself as she started to walk past.

For one thing, it was rude and intrusive. Two, she could care less what was going on inside. Sex or scrabble. Neither were her business.

At the same time, if Dillon really was having sex with Susie Wilcox, it meant that not only had he changed, but the town had let him. Somehow, someway, he'd killed a lifetime of perception in a matter of months.

And she couldn't help but wonder how he'd done it.

If he'd done it.

Curiosity burned through her and her footsteps slowed. She'd take one quick little peek and no one would be the wiser. Cupping her hands over her brow, she leaned toward the window.

She blinked and the dimly lit room started to focus. A pair of jeans lay in a heap on the hardwood floor. A lacey bra dangled over the back of a nearby leather chair. One red high heel peeked out from under the corner of the bed. The covers bunched at the bottom of the mattress, the bedspread a tangled heap on the floor.

A very naked Susie Wilcox lay on her stomach, her cheek nuzzling a pillow, one arm slung over her head, the other resting on the empty spot next to her—

Wait a second. Empty?

Just as the thought struck, she heard the deep, familiar voice. "Nice view."

The words slid into her ears and her heart stalled. The hair on the back of her neck prickled. Awareness zipped up and down her spine, along with a rush of embarrassment.

She was *so* busted.

3

SHE KNEW IT WAS DILLON even before she turned around.

Before her gaze swept from the long bare feet peeking from beneath the frayed hem of a worn pair of jeans, up denim-clad legs, past a trim waist and an enticing funnel of whiskey-colored hair that bisected washboard abs, over a muscular chest, thick biceps encircled by slave-band tattoos, a corded neck, to the familiar face—

Wait a minute.

Tattoos?

Her attention swiveled to one sinewy arm. Sure enough, an intricate black design snaked around the bulging muscle, making it seem larger and more powerful. Her gaze swiveled to the other arm. *Ditto.*

"Nice view," he repeated.

The deep timbre of his voice drew her full attention and made her tummy quiver. Her thighs trembled and her nipples pebbled and—

Girlfriend, puleeeeease. We're talking *Dillon*. The guy who'd given her dry-cleaning coupons for her last birthday. Other than those few ridiculous moments in anticipation (thanks to Kim and Mickey) of their first kiss, she'd never felt anything for him other than friendship.

Certainly *not* the overwhelming need to get hot and sweaty and naked.

Then again, she'd never seen him wearing nothing but worn, faded jeans, the top button undone, a pair of dark and dangerous tattoos and a relaxed, confident, sexy-as-hell smile.

"Yeah," she blurted, eager to distract herself from the sudden trembling of her body. "She's, um, really pretty." Her throat tightened around the words as if it actually bothered her to admit as much.

As if.

"I wasn't talking about the view inside." His gaze slid from her eyes to her mouth and lingered for several seconds.

If she hadn't known better, she would have sworn she felt a distinct pressure on her bottom lip. Like an invisible finger tracing the plump fullness, testing it... *Crazy.*

She licked her lips, killing the strange sensation, and his gaze collided with hers.

"I'm talking about the view out here," he added. Something hot and sensual shimmered in the green depths of his eyes and her pulse jumped.

"I've left over a dozen messages," she blurted, eager to ignore the sudden butterflies that fluttered away in her stomach. She gathered her indignation and nailed him with a stare. "Did you forget how to use a phone, or have you been avoiding me on purpose?"

The corner of his mouth crooked into the faintest hint of a smile. "I've been a little busy."

She glanced at the window. "Too busy to call your folks?" She eyed him. "I saw your mom at the hardware store last week. She's worried about you."

He shrugged, his biceps flexing. The tattoos encircling his arms seemed to widen. "I haven't been able to call."

"You haven't been able to, or you haven't wanted to?"

"Things are different for me now. I'm different. I doubt they'd understand."

Meg doubted it, too. They'd freaked out when he'd stepped in an ant bed back in the fifth grade and had pulled Doc Wilmer away from a championship golf game just to apply Benadryl. Meg could only imagine what they would do if they knew Dillon was stepping into motel rooms, and every place else it seemed, with every available woman in town.

Correction—almost every available woman. He'd been avoiding her like the plague.

"What's going on with you? You never miss pepperoni day." She didn't mean to sound so accusing. So what if he'd blown off their monthly lunch at Uncle Buck's Pizza not once, but twice now? She would have skipped their infamous double-decker pepperoni in a heartbeat in favor of a date with a really hot guy. "You could have at least called."

"I meant to." The sexy confidence faded for a split second and she glimpsed a twinkle of true regret. "Don't be mad."

"Because you're going through some major life crisis and didn't have the decency to tell me? You really think I'd be mad at a little thing like that?"

"You're not mad, then."

"I meant that sarcastically." He grinned and she felt her indignation melt. "Okay, spill it. What's up?"

He gave another shrug. "What can I say? I'm finally coming out of my shell."

"At thirty-one?"

"Maybe I'm a late bloomer."

"And maybe I'm wearing polyester to the next VFW dance." She shook her head. "It's more than that. Something happened to you."

"You've found me out." He leaned one hand on the window near her head and leaned down, his lips brushing her ear as he murmured, "I'm not really Dillon. I just look like him."

The scent of him, so raw and masculine, slid into her nostrils and filled her head. For a split second, she had the urge to lean closer, to press her lips to the side of his neck, to taste him with her tongue, to—

She fought the urge and leaned back.

"I suppose you're really a pod person and we're about to be invaded by little green men."

"They're purple, but you get the idea."

"You're so full of it." She leveled a stare at him. "I was really worried."

A strange gleam lit his eyes, but then it faded into a vivid green that sparkled and glittered so bright she found herself staring for the next few heartbeats until reality zapped some common sense into her and she managed to shift her attention to his mouth.

He had really great lips. Full, but not too full. Just right for a man.

She'd always thought so. At least for those few moments before he'd given her some of *the* worst kisses of her life.

He stiffened. "I'm sorry you were worried, but I can take care of myself." His sudden frown faded into an easygoing grin. "And most anyone else who comes along." The words were ripe with innuendo and her tummy did a quick somersault before hollowing out.

Dillon, she reminded herself. *Dry-cleaning. Zero attraction.*

But while her brain received the crucial messages loud and clear, her body had tuned in to a different frequency.

Warmth zipped up and down her spine, sending out blasts of heat to every erogenous zone in her body, from the arches of her feet and the sensitive skin below her belly button, to the ripened tips of her breasts and the back of each ear.

She had the sudden urge to step forward, close the fraction of distance between them and press her body flush against his.

So do it.

The words, raw and sexy, rumbled through her head as if Dillon himself stood next to her and murmured the encouragement directly in her ear.

He didn't. He stood inches away, his mouth crooked in a sinful grin, his eyes gleaming with desire and a knowing light that said he read every lascivious thought that raced through her mind.

Yeah. Sure.

She'd obviously had one too many of Winona's pleasure bites. No way would she ever make the first move on a man again.

Been there. Done that. Uh, uh.

And she certainly wouldn't make the first move on *Dillon,* of all people. He wasn't her type. He never had been. She went for tall, sexy, aggressive.

Okay, so maybe he *was* her type. All except for the aggressive part.

There were no strong purposeful hands reaching for her, no seeking lips. Gone was the uncertainty that had always simmered so hot and bright in his greener-than-green eyes when it came to women. The fear. Rather, his gaze blazed with a newfound confidence that did crazy things to her heartbeat.

He stood there, ready and waiting, as if he expected her to be overcome by lust and fall all over him.

"You did it, didn't you?" she blurted as the truth crystallized.

He arched one blond eyebrow. "You're the one looking through the window. You tell me."

His meaning sank in and her cheeks started to burn. Or maybe it was the sudden knowing gleam in his eyes that made her face heat. Either way, her body temperature climbed degree by dangerous degree with each passing second. "Not *it* as in sex," she said, managing to find her voice. "Although you obviously did that, too. I'm talking about you. You've really changed." Somehow, someway, Dillon Cash had managed to accomplish in a matter of months what she'd spent half her life trying to do. "You're really and truly—" she swallowed "—*sexy*."

His mouth slanted into a grin. "You say that like it's a bad thing."

"Not at all. It's really good. Great, in fact." She shook her head. "I just can't figure out how you did it. I mean, obviously, you did the whole makeover thing—" she eyed his jeans "—with the exception of the clothes, but it's more than that." Her gaze met his. "I've read every self-help sex book known to man. I've taken tons of seminars at the junior college. I've completed several online courses. This is my eighth class with Winona since she took over for Cheryl Anne." She shook her head. "And I'm still trying to get onto Tilly's list." She glanced through the handspan of window space at the beauty draped across the bed.

He'd done it, all right. He'd finally uncovered the secret she'd been searching for all these years—he'd found a way to make himself ultra attractive to the opposite sex.

Women ogled him. Fantasized about him. Stripped off their clothes and hopped into bed without a thought.

Skull Creek's biggest geek had become a bona fide sex object.

To every other woman, that is, except Meg.

She knew firsthand that people couldn't just change. Not deep down inside. Not overnight. It had taken her years to complete the process. There was no way he'd managed it in a matter of months.

No, he was still the same Dillon beneath the silky hair and toned muscles. Still the same guy who'd thrown up after Darla Sue Alcott had turned him down for the Homecoming dance.

She knew that, even if it was getting more difficult with each passing second to remember it.

A strange look crossed his face, as if he'd peeked into her head and glimpsed her thoughts. But then the expression faded into an easy grin and her heart gave a double thump.

"Six months ago, you couldn't even talk to a girl," she pointed out, her own desperation getting the better of her. "And now you've got Susie Wilcox offering herself to you like some pagan sacrifice."

"Talking's overrated," he said, his deep voice rumbling through her. "There are much more interesting ways to communicate."

"And you learned this how? Book? Seminar? Gene therapy that replaces geek DNA with a hung-like-a-horse chromosome?" The last comment drew a full-blown smile from him. "Because whatever it is, I want some."

He arched an eyebrow. "You want to be hung like a horse?"

"You know what I mean." Her gaze locked with his. "I want the female equivalent. I want to know your secret." A secret that would surely land her on Tilly's newest Hot Chicks list. If Meg could make the list, she had no doubt that the men in town would view her differently.

Bye, bye Manhandler Meg, hello irresistible sex object.

"You owe me," she told Dillon, "so pay up." When he gave

her a questioning look, she added, "For your half of the pizza, plus the tip. Add in pain and suffering because I had to sit there alone, and punitive damages to my hips because of all the extra calories I consumed since I don't believe in wasting, and I'd say you owe me big-time."

His gaze dropped. "Your hips look pretty good to me."

The butterflies started again. An insane reaction because the old Dillon had never acknowledged anything about her. Not her hips. Or her trim waist. Or even the decent rack she'd been showing off with a Wonderbra since senior year.

This Dillon seemed to notice everything.

And made her want to offer herself up as the second willing sacrifice of the night.

She shook away the sudden visual—Dillon naked and panting above her—that popped into her head and focused on her grumbling stomach. She hadn't eaten yet, so it was no wonder she was feeling so deprived.

She wanted food, not Dillon. Not really.

She swallowed and did a mental recitation of the menu at her favorite restaurant. "Good try, but you're not changing the subject. Give," she persisted.

"Since when did you get so bossy?"

"Since birth. Seriously, I want to know." Desperation bubbled inside of her, along with the deprivation niggling at her gut. "I *need* to know."

He eyed her for a long, drawn-out moment and she had the feeling that he faced some internal struggle.

"You're sure? You *really* want to know?" he finally asked.

Excitement rushed through her and she nodded. "Tell me *everything*."

"I've got a better idea." His gaze gleamed with a hidden knowledge. His fingers flexed on the glass next to her as he leaned forward. His stubbled jaw rasped her cheekbone. His lips grazed her ear. "Why don't I show you instead?"

4

WHAT THE HELL WAS HE thinking?

The thought pushed its way past the ferocious hunger that gripped Dillon's insides and sent a burst of reality straight to his brain.

This was Meg. His buddy. His pal. His friend.

Meg was the one woman he could actually talk to.

The only woman who'd ever cared what he had to say.

No way was he thinking about pushing her up against the nearest wall, sinking himself into her hot body and soaking up her delicious energy while he pumped in and out and drove her to a screaming climax.

And there was *no* way he was thinking about sinking his fangs into her sweet neck and drinking in her essence while he pumped in and out and drove her to a screaming climax.

While he fed off blood and sex, he never indulged in both at the same time. That was the first rule Garret, his other vampire mentor, had taught him. The big no-no because it forged a bond that was unbreakable. *Forever.*

The last thing Dillon wanted was to tie himself to one woman for the rest of eternity. Not when he was *this* close to breaking Bobby's record.

That's what he told himself, but with Meg's scent filling his nostrils and her frantic heartbeat echoing in his ears, forever didn't seem like such a long time. His muscles tightened and his gut ached and he had the sudden thought that he wanted her more than he wanted to break Bobby's record.

And she wanted a double pepperoni pizza with extra cheese.

The thought slid into his head and he pulled back. His gaze drilled into hers. Sure enough, he saw an image of Uncle Buck's Pizza Joint, a table, an extra large pie, and Meg scarfing it down to her heart's content.

She didn't want him.

Or at least, she didn't *want* to want him. She responded to him. All women did. But she wasn't falling all over him like every other woman he'd come into contact with in the past few months—with the exception of Nikki, the owner of the local beauty salon.

Nikki was totally enamored of Jake and so her lack of interest didn't bother Dillon.

But Meg… She was a single, red-blooded female. She should be out of her mind with lust.

Or at least a little overwhelmed.

He drank in the sight of her. No inviting smile. No come-and-get-me-now gaze. No pleading or begging.

"Please."

All right, so she was begging. A little. But not in the way he'd become accustomed to since stepping over to the vamp side. She wanted his help. His guidance. His advice.

What she didn't want was to jump into the sack with him.

Correction, she didn't want to want to jump into the sack with him. He stared into her bright gaze and read the truth as if it were spelled out in neon. She was determined to resist temptation, to wait for a man—any man—to make the first move when it came to sex. She was even more determined to resist Dillon. They had too much history. Even more, she knew for a fact—makeover aside—that he couldn't kiss worth a flip and she was in no hurry to try it again.

He fought down the urge to press his lips to hers and prove her wrong right then and there. He would have, if he hadn't been so determined to break Bobby's record.

Bobby hadn't put the moves on any woman. Rather, they'd come to him, eager and willing.

Ditto for every woman in Dillon's recent past. He was on a mission and he wasn't about to get distracted now.

"I've been trying to make Tilly's list forever," Meg continued. "If I can beef up my sex appeal, I'll be a shoe-in. You have to give me some pointers."

"And what will you give me?" He waited for a long list of seductive suggestions starting with "I'll strip naked and give you a lap dance."

"New clothes."

He blinked. "Excuse me?"

"While you've made a decent transformation physically and, obviously, mentally, what with overcoming your shyness and everything, you haven't come anywhere close to finding a sense of style." She eyed his jeans. "Designer?"

"Who cares?"

"The majority of women the world over, every homosexual on the face of the planet, and let's not forget the metrosexuals, bless their stylish little souls."

"When I look at a woman, I seriously doubt she cares what sort of jeans I'm wearing." He gave her an intense look and grinned at the way her pulse suddenly leapt at the base of her throat. But while the reaction was immediate and intense, it quickly faded and once again she was fantasizing about the pizza. "My jeans are irrelevant."

"Maybe. But if you're going to do something, you might as well do it right. Namely, if you want to make a complete transformation, it means looking the part right down to your skivvies." She arched an eyebrow. "You still doing the Spider-man boxers?"

"Not since the third grade." Her dad had gone out of town and she'd slept over at his house. She'd worn an oversize Green Bay Packers T-shirt that night, while he'd been in his webbed boxers and a plain white T-shirt. She'd brought her army men and a flashlight, and they'd snuck into his closet after bedtime and played until dawn. While she'd looked and acted like one of the boys back then, she'd smelled a hundred times better. He could still remember the scent of her strawberry shampoo.

His nostrils flared. Beneath the perfume and hair products, he caught a whiff of the familiar scent.

"Whites?" she persisted. "Solids?"

"Neither." He inhaled again and electricity spiraled straight to his groin. He fought against the hunger and focused on giving her another grin. "I'm in commando mode."

"Oh." Her gaze shifted nervously and he knew she was racing to think of something else to say to distract herself from the sudden mental image he'd stirred. She shrugged. "Okay, so you don't really need any advice when it comes to undergarments. But these jeans..." She shook her head and wrinkled her nose.

"There's nothing wrong with them."

"They're from last year's bargain bin at the Shop-'til-you-drop, aren't they?"

"So?"

"So you need a pair that are a little more updated, not to mention a shirt to go with them. An outfit that says cool, classy, sexy, which I can certainly provide." She leveled a blazing blue stare at him and made her proposition. "You educate me in the finer points of being a convincing sex object, and I'll help you find a look that does your new image some justice."

He seriously doubted she could come up with anything that could do more for his sex appeal than the vamp blood flowing through his veins, but the thought of letting her try definitely snagged his attention.

Resisting him during a brief run-in like this might be easy. But no way could she hold back if they spent more than five minutes together. The thought struck and suddenly he knew exactly what he needed to do—seduce Meg Sweeney to the point that she stopped holding back and offered herself to him like the countless other females in Skull Creek.

Not only would he break Bobby's record, but he would disprove beyond a doubt what he'd started to suspect—that he was, indeed, as geeky as everyone thought.

Tempting a woman determined not to be tempted would be

the ultimate proof, not to mention he'd spent a lot of years wishing he could go back and re-do that first horrific kiss.

His memory stirred and he saw the disappointment in her eyes, the reluctance to try it again.

The image fueled his determination and he gave her his most seductive smile. "You've got yourself a deal, darlin'."

DARLIN'? SINCE WHEN DID Dillon Cash use the term *darlin'*?

Since he's morphed into a megalicious stud-muffin who makes you want to rip off your panties and do the happy dance all over him.

Not that she would.

She was through taking the lead. She wanted a man to want her so badly that he couldn't keep his hands off of her. A man who would gladly rip off *his* boxers and do the happy dance all over *her*.

Holding tight to her resolve, she drew a deep breath and concentrated on putting one foot in front of the other as she walked back toward the motel lobby.

She could feel his gaze on her and awareness zipped through her. Her nipples pebbled and she became painfully aware of the way the lace cups of her bra rubbed back and forth with the slight swinging motion of her arms. Her blue jean skirt tugged and pulled and her thighs actually trembled.

Thanks to Dillon and his suddenly overwhelming sex appeal.

As tempting as he was, she couldn't deny her good fortune. She'd definitely found the key to her future success. Once they started lessons—

Her thoughts slammed to a halt. She'd been so anxious to escape her traitorous thoughts that she hadn't proposed a time and date for their first session.

"What about tomorrow morning—" she said, but the words died as she turned and found the walkway empty.

June bugs bumped against the single bulb that lit the concrete path. Her gaze traveled back to the spot where he'd stood and she eyed the closed door.

No rustle of denim as he'd turned. No creak of metal as he'd opened the door…. No thud as the door had shut behind him. Nothing.

One minute, she'd felt his gaze and the next…*poof*. He'd disappeared.

Right.

She ignored the strange tingling that worked its way up her spine. He wasn't actually *gone*. He was inside and she'd obviously been too wound up in her thoughts and her body's traitorous response to notice the details.

Grasping at the explanation, she fought down the notion that something wasn't quite right and turned back toward the lobby.

She would give him a call in the morning and set up a meeting. Maybe midmorning. While she didn't have any men's clothes in her shop, she could take his measurements and then do some online shopping later. He would tell her what books he'd been reading, give her some pointers, and then they could head over to Uncle Buck's for a makeup lunch.

Thanks to her lustful thoughts and her desperate attempt for a diversion, she had a sudden craving for double pepperoni that even a dozen pleasure bites couldn't touch.

A craving that haunted her for the next hour as she turned in her homework, finished her class and headed home. A craving that drove her straight to her kitchen in search of satisfaction, aka junk food.

In massive quantities if possible.

Since it was the end of the week and she hadn't yet made it to the grocery store, she quickly ruled out *massive* and settled for Babe's three remaining Twinkies. She also snatched up what was left of a bottle of wine she'd received from one of her customers the Christmas before last.

Bottle in one hand and sponge cake in the other, she headed upstairs and tried not to think about Dillon and whether or not he'd improved in the kissing department.

Obviously, he had. Otherwise, he wouldn't have every woman in town falling all over him.

Most of the women in town, that is.

They were just friends, she told herself as she peeled off her clothes and crawled into bed.

Just like she saw the real Dillon, he saw the real Meg. The one who hadn't managed to cancel her subscription to *Sports Illustrated*. The one who still tossed around a baseball in the back-yard every now and then when she was sure her neighbors weren't looking.

Which explained why he'd done little more than flirt with her tonight. Not that she'd wanted him to do more.

It was the principle that mattered.

Obviously, like everyone else in town, he just couldn't see the Hot Chick that Meg had become.

Not yet.

Not ever a voice whispered. One she quickly ignored as she devoured two of the three cakes, downed a long sip of wine and snuggled under the sheets.

If Dillon could convince an entire town full of people he'd known since birth, so could she. Even more, she could be convincing enough to get herself into Tilly's top ten.

All she had to do was buckle down, learn everything she could from Dillon, and *not* jump his bones in the process.

No problem. Manhandler Meg was ancient history.

At least that's what she told herself.

5

SHE NEEDED HIM TO SEX her up.

Even more, she *wanted* him to sex her up.

Dillon sat in the small office that housed the administrative portion—aka a desk, a file cabinet and a state-of-the-art computer system—of Skull Creek Choppers and tried to push Meg and her proposition completely out of his head.

The truth echoed through his head, tightening his groin and stirring the damned need that twisted his gut. He fought against the sensations and tried to focus. He had work to do. He was smack-dab in the middle of developing custom-design software for a new line of choppers being introduced in the Fall.

He'd spent the past hour since leaving the motel hard at work on the templates that would be the starter point for each bike. At the moment, Jake and Garret were working from a sketch only, crafting the cycles from the ground up and dealing with problems as they arose during the building process. The computer program Dillon was developing would simplify everything and allow them to foresee any structural and/or mechanical problems before they encountered them. They would be able to enter in the measurements and must-haves for each bike. The computer would process the information and put together a cyber model, pinpointing errors and "fixing" them before any actual fabrication. Dillon was just days away from putting the final touches on the program, which meant he didn't need a distraction right now.

He stared at a particular line of code, but instead of seeing the sequence of numbers and letters, he saw Meg, her lips so full and kissable, her blue eyes filled with determination.

A sliver of excitement went through him, followed by a wave of disbelief. He still couldn't grasp the fact that she'd asked for his help. Thanks to his ability to read minds, he now knew she never asked a man for anything.

Never demanded or pushed or manhandled.

Not anymore.

She'd sworn off any and all aggressive behavior when it came to sex. She wanted a man to lust after her. She wanted to feel desirable and sexy and confident that her own transformation—from pudgy tomboy to curvaceous woman—had been successful.

Deep down, she wasn't so sure.

He'd seen the truth in her gaze, the way he saw everything else about her—she was up to her neck in mortgage payments on her dream house, she had a dog addicted to Twinkies, she loved her job even if it did mean being cooped up most of the day and, thanks to the upcoming prom season, she was certain she would double her profits this year.

Yes, he saw it all. Her hopes. Her dreams. Her fears—the biggest being that she was doomed to a lifetime of being Manhandler Meg, regardless of how much she tried to change things.

Which was why she'd asked for help. She needed him.

Him, of all people.

The sudden burst of skepticism made him all the more confident in his own decision. He would help her, all right, and teach her his "secret."

Not that he was going to sink his fangs into her sweet neck and bring her over to the dark side, not when he had zero intention of staying there himself. He would never do that. He wasn't sure he even could. He was still learning the ropes from Garret and that wasn't something the older vampire had ever addressed.

But while he wouldn't turn her, he *would* teach her what he'd learned about seduction since his own turning.

One of the key factors that made vamps such sensual creatures was that they were fine-tuned to everything. They saw things more vividly, smelled them more intensely. They were aware of even the smallest sound, the briefest touch. While Meg's senses weren't supercharged like his, she still had them. If she learned to tap into them more, to use them, trust them, he had no doubt it would boost her sex appeal tenfold.

Enough to make her irresistible to every man in town.

The notion stirred a rush of jealousy. Understandable, of course. They were friends. It only made sense that he would feel protective of her. That, and he felt even more aroused than usual because she wasn't throwing herself at him like every other woman he met. She knew the real Dillon, which made her all the more determined *not* to sleep with him. Which made him all the more determined to sleep with her.

Thanks to free will, humans were much more powerful than they realized. While a vampire could, indeed, mesmerize and hypnotize, such supernatural persuasion meant a hill of beans if the subject wasn't willing.

Most women wanted to be swept away by passion. Deep down, they longed to experience wild, earth-shattering sex with a charismatic stranger, and so they were wide-open and vulnerable to his seduction.

Meg wasn't much different from every woman in that respect, and that was the problem in a nutshell. Dillon wasn't a stranger and so the last thing, the very last thing she wanted was wild, earth-shattering sex with him.

If he could seduce her to the point that she saw past the geek he used to be and embraced the hunk he'd become, he would know deep down inside that he truly had been acting all these years. That he wasn't a loser when it came to women.

That he wasn't a loser, period.

Seducing her would be the ultimate validation.

Excitement rippled through him. The scent of her strawberry shampoo spiraled through his head and hunger gnawed in his gut.

His mouth watered and his muscles tightened and it was all he could do to keep his ass in the chair.

He had to get a grip and take things slowly. One lesson at a time. Until she reached the point of no return. It might take a day. It might take a week. But eventually she would offer herself to him. Of that he felt certain.

In the meantime, it was business as usual.

He spent another fifteen minutes working on the code before closing the design screen and moving on to his second order of business—keeping his promise to Jake and Garret.

He stared through the wall of windows that separated the office from the fabrication shop. Jake McCann stood near a large metal table that held the skeleton of what would soon be the next custom chopper to roll through the doors of the motorcycle shop. Unlike most of the bikes they'd been doing, this one wasn't headed for a specific individual. Rather, it was a spec model being sent up north to advertise Skull Creek Choppers to the rest of the country. Jake took a few measurements before walking back over to another table that held a sheet of metal that would soon be the gas tank. He reached for a special tool and started tracing out the measurements.

Like most every other man in the small Texas town, Jake wore cowboy boots, jeans, a faded Resistol and an easygoing grin. But unlike most every other man in town, Jake was the real deal. A bona fide cowboy who'd been turned back in the eighteen hundreds. He'd spent his human life and a good chunk of his afterlife riding and working horses for a living. In the past decade or so, he'd traded in his horse for a hog. He was now one of the best cut-and-design guys in the chopper business. He was also deeply in love with Nikki Braxton, owner of the town's most popular beauty salon. Nikki was nice and beautiful and still very human. And she was staying that way as far as Jake was concerned.

As long as there was hope of finding and destroying Garret's sire.

Dillon's gaze shifted to the second man clad in jeans, a white T-shirt with a skull and cross bones on the front, and biker boots. He stood in the far corner near a large welding unit. He had a red, white and blue bandana tied around his head, a worn straw Resistol perched on top, and a pair of goggles secured over his eyes. Gloved hands reached for a long strip of metal. He powered on the ARC Unit and worked at the piece, firing and shaping until it started to resemble a rear fender.

Despite the hat, Garret wasn't anywhere close to a real cowboy. When he'd been turned back in the seventeen hundreds, he'd been a Texas patriot. A bona fide hero, and one of the founding fathers of Skull Creek. Not that anyone in town knew his identity. No, they thought he was just another leather-clad biker who'd invaded their small town to set up a manufacturing shop for his business. He liked fast motorcycles and even faster women, and he'd become somewhat of a role model for Dillon. The older vampire had been teaching him about his new vampness, showing him the ropes and outlining the vampire equivalent of the Ten Commandments.

Number one? No entering a home unless invited by the host. Public buildings were fair game, from the Piggly Wiggly to the local VFW Hall, but no personal dwellings unless specifically asked.

Number two—no direct sunlight.

Number three—no sharp objects, including knives, stakes and giant toothpicks like the ones used over at the Pig in the Poke Barbecue Joint.

Number four—no Italian restaurants. The old legend about garlic warding off vampires had turned out to be true. While it couldn't kill one of Dillon's kind, it could cause a lot of pain.

Number five—no solid food.

Number six—no changing eye colors. A vampire tended to reflect his emotions with his eyes and so they changed color frequently depending on his mood. Most vampires could control this. Since Dillon was young (in vamp years), he wasn't able to leash his feelings as easily as his older vamp buddies, but he was learning.

Number seven—no changing into a bat. Such a change took its toll and made the vampire weak and vulnerable. Which meant it was usually avoided.

Number eight—no indulging in blood and sex at the same time. Unless he wanted to tie himself to one woman for the rest of eternity. Talk about a snowball's chance in hell. Dillon had waited too long to unleash the wildness inside. He wasn't screwing things up by landing himself in a permanent relationship.

Number nine—no spending more than one night with any one woman. The more sex a vampire had with a woman, the more she wanted him. The last thing any vampire needed was a *Fatal Attraction* chasing him all over town.

Which led to number ten—keeping a low profile. A vampire's survival hinged on blending in with mainstream society, laying low and playing it cool.

Hence Garret's cowboy hat. The vamp was now living in a small Texas town, and *When in Rome*, as the saying went.

While Garret taught the importance of blending and urged Dillon to accept what he'd become, the vampire didn't seem all that content in his own skin.

Rather, he seemed restless.

Anxious.

Hungry.

But not for sex and blood. No, Garret wanted what Jake wanted—his humanity.

Dillon turned his attention back to the computer and clicked on his Internet Explorer. A few seconds later, he logged in at MeetVamps.com and scrolled down the screen to the first comment posted on his page yesterday.

Lovrgrlvamp: Hey, there, Skull Creek. I'm not wearing any panties and it's soooo hot. I'm here waiting for u, baby.

O-kay. It wasn't exactly what he had had in mind when he'd signed up and started blogging a few weeks ago—to get some sort of lead on the Ancient One—but at least he had visitors. Not that he really thought the father of all vamps would be chatting online, but it was all he'd been able to think of to track down the vampire who'd sired Garret.

The same vampire who held the key to humanity for all three of them.

Destroying the source would reverse the curse for Garret and anyone that he'd turned, which meant Jake and Dillon would be free, as well.

As much as Dillon liked being a vampire, he knew he couldn't stay that way. He'd caused his parents enough grief, which was why he'd yet to break the news about his new fanged status. He was hoping he wouldn't have to. The blogging had given him a few leads so far—a couple of names and locations that he was busy following up on. With any luck, he would gather even more information and, eventually, hit the jackpot. Once he located the Ancient One, Dillon would help the other two vamps destroy him. Then he would embrace his humanity once again and go back to playing the town geek.

The notion sent a wave of anxiety through him and made him all the more eager to break Bobby's record. Because he knew that this was it. His one chance to prove the truth to himself and build enough memories to last him through all the long, lonely human nights that lay ahead.

It was now or never.

He tensed, raking stiff fingers through his hair. His groin throbbed and he shifted in the leather seat. He was wound tight. Hungry. Starving even.

You should have gone for round two with Miss Hot Chick.

That's what he usually did. What he'd been doing since he'd come to understand what he'd become and learned the all-important fact that sex was as crucial a sustenance as blood. More so because feeding off sexual energy curbed the need for blood. Sure, he still had to feed in the traditional sense, but not nearly as often.

All the more reason he should have gone for an all-nighter.

He'd meant to, but when he'd walked back into the motel room after Meg and her proposition, he hadn't been able to push either out of his head. And while he'd turned into an oversexed, greedy vampire, he wasn't a two-timing, oversexed greedy vampire.

He hadn't been able to make himself get busy with one woman while thinking about another.

Which meant he wasn't anywhere close to being satisfied.

He raked another hand through his hair and took a long sip of the ice-cold beer sitting on the desk next to him. It did little to relieve the heat burning him up from the inside out.

He forced his attention back to the screen and read his own post. He'd been trying to spark somebody's memory.

SkullCreekVamp: I had the dream again. The details were so clear that I'm starting to think that it's not a dream at all, but the real deal. I'm remembering what happened to me. The pain. The hunger. The presence. Anybody else remember details? I want to remember a face, but I can't. Not yet.

Of course, that wasn't true. Dillon knew exactly who was responsible for his current state—Jake. The older vamp had turned him in a desperate attempt to give him back the life that had been ripped away when Garret had inadvertently attacked him. It had been the anniversary of Garret's turning and he'd been instinctively called back to the place of his death to relive those few moments when his humanity had slipped away. Like any vampire going through the turning, he'd been out of control. Mindless. Dillon had gotten in his way. He'd be six feet under right now if Jake hadn't intervened and turned him before it was too late.

Dillon would never forget that moment. The anguish at feeling his life slipping away, the excitement when he'd drank from Jake and new life had rushed back through him, strong and more potent than anything he'd ever felt before.

Likewise, Jake remembered his own sire—Garret.

Garret was the only member of the vamp trio who couldn't remember. Sure, he had a few images and impressions that had lingered in the two hundred years since he'd been turned in what was now the town square, but nothing clear when it came to the vamp responsible. One minute he'd been heading home after fighting for Texas independence, and the next he'd been attacked by a band of Mexican bandits. They'd robbed and killed him, or so the history books said. But someone—something—had happened along and changed all of that. One of the bandits? Maybe. Maybe not. He didn't know. There'd been no formal "Hi, I'm so-and-so, the ancient vampire who's going to turn you instead of leaving your dying carcass to rot." Rather, one minute he'd been following the light into the hereafter, and the next that light had been obliterated by a shadow looming over him. He remembered the pain ripping through his body, the smell—sweet, intense, intoxicating—that had filled his head, and a gold medallion.

Dillon glanced at the small sketch Garret had made of the piece of jewelry. He was hoping to gather a little info on some recent turnings to see if he could find a newly turned vampire who remembered the same gold pendant. If so, maybe the new vamp would remember even more—a physical description, maybe even a name.

He scrolled down the screen, his gaze drinking in the various posts.

Wannabevamp: Stop worrying about the f@#$%^& dream and just enjoy. I would give anything to turn. I tried the new enamel fangs and while they worked pretty well, they're nothing like the real thing.

Vamp4Life: Pain is a state of mind. A place you visit. If you choose not to go, then you're home free and you don't have anything to worry about. That, or you can try a Vicodin. Or even Xanax. Both work for me.

DarkAngel: So what if there was pain? The trick is not to fight it. Embrace the feeling, relish it, worship it. It's who you are. Who we are.

BradtheImpaler: Got 3 prs of fangs. This really rad dentist in Queens made them 4 me and they're sharp as hell. I get a discount on my next pair if I send him a referral. Wannabe, if ur up near Queens, want me to hook u up?

Fangtastic: I sell some high quality incisors if anyone's inter-

ested. I'm even a preferred seller on eBay. I offer free shipping, too, if you order more than one pair. I also have some really cool vampire porn.

Lovrgrlvamp: I like pain. Spankings are my favorite. Maybe we should get together and whip each other. I'm game if you're ever out the Chicago way. Or maybe I could head down to Texas. Whip me, cowboy. Whip me gooooooooood...

He read the rest of the comments—most of which, with the exception of Dark Angel, were ripe with sexual innuendo and tips for going vamp—before posting his next entry where he mentioned the location of his turning (also Garret's) and the timing (over two hundred years ago). He was just powering off his computer when Jake opened the glass door and ducked his head inside the office.

"Hey, bud, can you help me out for a second? I want to fit the new tank in place and I need an extra pair of hands."

"Sure thing." Dillon followed Jake into the shop and helped hold the tank in place so the vamp could take more measurements.

Then he spent the next few hours learning the finer art of tank shaping. A good thing since he was desperate for a distraction from the need gnawing at his belly and the sudden vision of Meg—her naked body stretched out beneath him, her eyes glazed with passion, her bottom lip full and swollen from his kisses, her breasts flushed, her nipples hard and greedy, her body so warm and wet—that stuck in his brain.

But the more he trailed his fingers over the warm, smooth metal, kneading and shaping, the more the vision turned to a full-blown fantasy.

He felt her warm skin beneath his hands. Her breasts, hot and flushed, pressed against his chest. Her mouth ate at his. Her body sucked at his cock...

Shit. He wanted her now.

Not tomorrow when they met for their first lesson.

Not a few days from now after he'd seduced her to the point that she no longer resisted the attraction between them.

Not next week after they'd had a chance to spend more time together and she fell hook, line and sinker for his vamp charisma.

Now.

The need ate away inside of him as he finished the tank and finally called it a night. He had little more than an hour until daylight. Plenty of time to head out to Garret's place.

He'd been staying with the older vampire at a large ranch on the outskirts of town now that his own house was off-limits. While he had a pretty secluded place, he had far too many windows for comfort. There was also the fact that his parents were camped out in his front yard, hell-bent on deprogramming him from whatever cult he'd fallen in with.

Garret's ranch house had an old wine cellar that provided a dark, safe place to sleep during the day. The spread was also sizable, which afforded plenty of seclusion.

He climbed onto his motorcycle and kicked the bike to life. He sped out of the parking lot with every intention of turning east toward the ranch.

Only his hands seemed to have a mind of their own as they hung a sharp left and headed west. He opened up the engine. The bike screamed toward the center of town and the small two-story colonial that sat a few blocks over from Main Street.

He went left again, then right. His headlamp cast wicked shadows across the pavement as the motorcycle ate up the distance to the brick structure that sat several houses down from the corner.

Easing his bike over to the curb on the opposite side of the street, he killed the engine. The motor sizzled and hissed, the faint noise blending in with the buzz of crickets and a dozen other sounds that drifted on the cool April breeze. Sounds barely discernable to anyone but Dillon.

Since he'd been turned it was as if someone had upped the amp level in his brain. He heard *everything*—the snores of an old couple several houses down, the obnoxious voice of the host of some infomercial blazing from a nearby neighbor's television set, the rustling of cans and paper as a raccoon clawed through a trash can, the steady *shhhhhhhh* as someone took a whiz in their john.

He fixed his gaze on the house surrounded by a white picket fence and overflowing flower beds. A large wraparound porch spanned the bottom level. A swing sat at the far corner. The second level had a wraparound balcony filled with potted plants and white wicker patio furniture.

It was far from the small log cabin Meg had shared with her father before his death, but then Dillon knew that was the idea— to bury the past and forget. This place had lots of windows and French doors and bright yellow trim. It looked as feminine as the woman who now lived inside it. Her car sat in the driveway, the brand-new yellow Mustang convertible, a far cry from the old brown Chevy pickup she'd driven her junior year of high school. The car was flashy, sexy, exciting.

Just like Meg.

He'd always thought so, even way back when she'd driven the truck. He'd just never had the courage to tell her, particularly after those disastrous first kisses.

The house was one of the oldest in town, built sometime back in the 1800s before central air and heat. A portable air-conditioning unit sat in the window near a set of French doors on the second story. The engine purred steadily until Dillon narrowed his gaze. He felt the heat rush through his body as he sent the silent command. The motor coughed and sputtered. The *purrrrr* turned to a distinctive whine.

The minutes ticked off one by one, as he waited for Meg to appear in the doorway.

She was yards away, the room where she stood completely black, yet he saw every detail. She wore only a pink T-shirt and lace panties. Sweat dotted her brow and beaded on her skin as she threw the lock. Hauling open the doors, she stood there framed in the double doorway, the sheer curtains billowing behind her as she drank in the fresh night air. She took several deep breaths and her frustration mounted.

She needed more relief than the cool breeze whispering through the trees.

She'd been sleeping alone with the exception of a bright red vibrator she kept in her top nightstand drawer and she was desperate. She needed a real man, and she needed him soon.

The thought carried on the breeze, through the trees and across the pavement. It slid into his brain where he stood yards away.

Watching.

Waiting.

Wanting.

Hunger gripped him, a fierce ache that started in his gut and spread through his entire body, making him tremble and shake. And suddenly it didn't matter who came on to who. He wanted to touch her. He needed to.

He was going to.

Right. *Now.*

6

SHE NEEDED TO DITCH THE failing window unit, take a bite out of her savings and invest in central air-conditioning.

Meg came to that conclusion as she stood in the doorway and welcomed the faint rush of wind that whispered over her flushed skin. She'd been tapped out after paying the down payment on her dream home, and rather than replace the major appliances, she'd tried to get away with repairing and refurbishing.

In the five years since buying her place, she'd fixed the upstairs unit not once, but four times now.

The air conditioner grumbled and growled.

Make that five.

She made a mental note to call Mr. Abel, the air conditioning guy, first thing in the morning and moved on to the next window in the room. A few seconds later, she had all three of the room's windows wide-open. Air filtered through the space, relieving some of the stifling heat that had pulled her from sleep.

Then again, it hadn't been just the heat that had kept her from nodding off. She'd spent the better part of the past hour tossing and turning, trying to push Dillon Cash completely out of her head.

So what if he was sexy now? And handsome? And—with the exception of his clothes—had the whole hot-guy thing going? He was still just Dillon. Her buddy. Her pal. The guy who'd given her *the* worst kiss of her entire life.

Sure, he appeared convincing, but she knew better. She wasn't the least bit hot and bothered by his new image.

She *wasn't*.

Ignoring a sudden ripple of awareness that drifted down her spine, she walked back over to the bed. She cast a quick glance at the open doorway. Moonlight spilled onto the balcony, illuminating the potted azaleas, the small white wicker table and matching chairs, a swaying wind chime. The soft *ting ting* echoed in her ears. Everything looked and sounded the same, yet she couldn't escape the sudden inexplicable feeling that something was different.

That someone—or something—was there with her.

For a split second, she saw a tall, muscular figure standing near the rails, the broad shadow edged in moonlight.

Her heart kick-started and she blinked. Just like that, the image disappeared.

She ignored the sudden drumming in her chest, walked back over to her bed, stretched out on top of the covers and clamped her eyes shut. Her hormones were definitely getting the best of her. She was so wound up, so desperate for some male company that she was starting to imagine it.

A man on her balcony.

If only.

Forcing a deep breath, she focused on the steady rise and fall of her chest. *Up. Down. In. Out…* Soon, the tension in her body slipped away. Her muscles went lax and her mind grew fuzzy.

She was this close to dozing off when a sudden gust of wind rushed through the window and the curtains billowed and snapped.

Her eyes popped open and her skin prickled. Goose bumps danced along her arms. She reached for the lamp and a blaze of light chased away the shadows. Her gaze ping-ponged from one corner of the room to the next, but there was no one there. Just a dresser overflowing with cosmetics, a stand-up mirror, a pile of undies she hadn't had the time to fold and a stack of new fall fashion catalogs from various distributors.

She killed the light, wiggled her way under the sheet and clamped her eyes shut again. She forced aside the sudden image of Dillon that popped into her head—his bright gaze green and blazing, his mouth crooked into a killer smile—and concentrated on mentally reciting tomorrow's schedule.

She had the Weatherby twins for a prom fitting at ten. Elise Harwell and her youngest daughter at eleven. Melissa Sue Jones and her four bridesmaids at noon. Melissa Sue's mother at one. Old Mrs. Cromwell at two-thirty… While she had an idea what she was going to show the twins and Melissa Sue, she was at a loss for Elise. While she'd seen the woman's youngest daughter around town, she'd never actually met her face-to-face. She had no clue what colors the girl liked or what sort of styles she might be interested in. At the same time, she couldn't be all that different from her four older sisters who were the spitting image of their well-groomed, fashion-conscious mother. Elise lived for the latest trends and hottest colors.

By the time Meg had mentally rifled through her newest selections and narrowed them down to a handful of the most chic possibilities, her heart had slowed and her nerves had calmed. Peace seeped through her, pushing away consciousness and muffling the whine of the failing air conditioner, the *tick-tock* of her bedside clock, the occasional *snap* and *pop* of the window sheers.

She was *this close* to conking out completely when she felt the faint pull and tug on the cotton sheet.

She cracked open one eye in time to see the sheet slither south, down her legs, to puddle around her ankles. The wind whispered over her toes. The sensation crept higher, feathering over her calves, her knees, her thighs. The edge of her T-shirt lifted and the hem slid upward, baring a pair of silky pink panties, several inches of pale skin, her navel, more skin, the undersides of her breasts. Her nipples tightened. The material snagged and caught on the ripe tips.

Her breath caught, her chest rose and her breasts strained against the fabric. It was a highly unsettling sensation. Erotic. Forbidden. *Impossible!*

Her other eye opened and she watched in stunned amazement as the material lifted, easing over her nipples, exposing the throbbing peaks. The edge of the shirt bunched as if invisible fingers tugged at the thin covering—

She clamped her eyes shut as her heart started to pound.

The wine. It had to be the wine.

She'd never been much of a drinker, which was why the bottle had lasted her over a year. She'd used it primarily for cooking and had indulged in the occasional glass with dinner. But never right before bed. And with a Twinkie chaser.

Sugared and sloshed. That was the problem. No wonder she was imagining things. The sheet. The T-shirt. The man framed in the doorway—

Wait a second.

She blinked and for a split second, she saw the familiar green eyes and sensuous mouth, but then the image blurred and faded.

Uh, yeah. Because he's not real. No way is Dillon Cash standing on your balcony. You're sloshed and hallucinating, end of story.

No more wine, she vowed, tugging her shirt down and yanking the sheet back up. She clamped her eyes shut. A dream. That's all it had been. A crazy, bizarre dream brought on by too much sugar and alcohol.

A crazy, bizarre, semi-pleasant dream, she admitted several minutes later, her body still buzzing from the sensation of fabric gliding this way and that. She drew a deep breath. Her nipples rubbed against the cotton of her T-shirt and her breasts tingled.

Okay, so maybe there was something to be said for a good Chardonnay and a couple of Twinkies right before bed.

On that stirring thought, she drifted into a deep sleep, not the least bit alarmed when the sheet started to glide down and her T-shirt started to inch its way up.

Again.

HE COULDN'T ACTUALLY touch her.

The truth crystallized as he stood in the open doorway and tried to step over the threshold. An invisible wall barred his way and refused to give him access to the tempting woman stretched out on the bed. Her T-shirt was up under her arms, her luscious breasts full and flushed, the sheet bunched down at her feet. Her skin was pale and soft looking against the pastel green sheets. His gaze went to the skimpy panties she wore. Not even a wisp of hair pushed through the scant lace and he knew the skin beneath was as smooth and as bare as the rest of her.

His mouth watered and his hands trembled. He could feel the need vibrating from her lush body. It called to him, begging him forward, tempting him until he shook with the force of it.

Wake her up, a voice whispered. *She'll invite you in.*

If she were every other women in town.

She wasn't. She was the one woman, the only woman who'd managed to resist him. That was why tonight wasn't about sating his own hunger.

It was about stirring hers.

He held tight to the thought and stiffened against his own urges.

Focusing his attention on the nearly empty wine bottle, he narrowed his gaze and sent a mental command. The bottle lifted, floating from the nightstand until it hovered over her full breasts. He gave the slightest motion of his head and the bottle tilted. A trickle of wine splashed over one nipple and her eyes popped open.

Panic chased confusion across her expression as her gaze darted between the wine bottle and the open doorway where he stood. Her gaze collided with his.

Relax. He sent the mental command and hoped that she would be too exhausted, too half-asleep to refuse. Her eyes widened, her lips parted and he had the fleeting thought that she was going to scream.

It's just a dream. He sent the silent thought and she caught her bottom lip. Her eyes glazed with need. *A fantasy,* he added. *So sit back and enjoy yourself.*

Her eyelids fluttered closed and her body relaxed.

He shifted his attention back to the wine bottle and watched as the glass tilted again. Another trickle splashed over her nipple and dribbled down the side of her breast to dampen the sheet beneath her.

The tip pebbled, responding to the sensation, begging for more. Her body arched, seeming to strain for more of the sensation, but she didn't open her eyes this time.

Because it was just a fantasy to her.

A very vivid, very erotic figment of her imagination.

The realization sent a rush of relief through him—he wasn't in a hurry to blow his cover and dodge a lynch mob—followed by a wave of irritation. Because as much as he liked being the star of her erotic musings, he wanted her fully awake and conscious when she gave herself to him.

The thought plagued him a full second before she drank in a deep breath and her chest lifted. Her nipple quivered and his gaze went to the faint blue vein barely visible beneath the translucent skin near one areola. Pain splintered his head and he felt the sharpness of his teeth against his tongue. His cock throbbed.

From the corner of his eye, he caught his reflection and saw the deep purple glow of his gaze. He stiffened, fighting against the emotion whirling inside of him until his eyes brightened into a rich vivid green.

Easy.

The command whispered through his head and he held tight to his control. He shifted his attention back to the wine bottle. The glass dipped until the edge grazed one of her ripe nipples. She gasped. The sound sizzled across the open space between them and slid into his ears, stirring what lived and breathed inside of him. A rush of longing pulsed from her flushed body and suddenly he knew beyond a doubt that she hadn't been with a man in one hell of a long time.

The realization sent a strange rush of satisfaction through him and made him all the more determined to resist his own damned hunger and satisfy hers.

The bottle tilted, drip-dropping wine over her bare stomach.

The rosy liquid pooled in her navel, slid decadently toward her lace panties and turned the white edge a pale pink.

She moaned and he moved lower, dribbling a little more here, a little more there, until the bottle was completely empty and her panties were damp with wine and her own need.

He trailed the cool edge of the bottle down the outside of one bare leg, up the inside of her knee, her thigh, building the anticipation until he reached the lacy barrier between her legs. He rubbed the mouth of the container up and down against the already drenched material. She gasped and wiggled her hips for more.

He felt his own gaze burn as he willed the scrap of lace down her legs until it tugged free of her ankles and feet and collapsed on the bed beside her.

Her thighs fell open, giving him an unobstructed view of the slick, pouty folds that begged for his attention.

At the first touch of the cool glass against her soft, tender slit, her eyelids fluttered open again.

She gazed first at the bottle between her legs and then at him. There was an instant of confusion and panic, and then the feelings eased into a glaze of passion as she smiled and mumbled, "No wonder Babe likes Twinkies."

He rubbed her with the bottle as her heavy gaze drank in his face, burning a path over his shoulders, his chest, down to the prominent erection that threatened to bust out of his jeans. Her attention lingered and the urge to step inside the room, shove his zipper down, spread her legs and sink into her wet body nearly overwhelmed him.

He couldn't and so he stared at her, into her, willing her eyes shut again. Finally, she complied, leaning her head back into the softness of the pillow as she gave in to the rush of sensation.

He continued the stroking, up and down, side to side until a drop of warmth spilled from her slick folds and slid down the neck of the dark glass. Her back arched and she came up off the bed. A breathy moan sailed past her lips as a wave of ecstasy crashed over her.

Watching her body tighten and pulse was almost as satisfying as relishing it firsthand. He could practically feel the rush of warmth as she milked him.

His erection throbbed and he felt the bubbling warmth that pulsed along its length, along with something else. A prickling awareness at the base of his spine that told him his time was nearly up.

Gathering his last shred of control, he drank in one last look at her and forced himself away from the doorway. Without a sound, he scaled the waist-high rail and dropped to the ground. In the blink of an eye, he covered the distance to his bike.

A faint glow tinged the horizon as he straddled the seat and gunned the engine. A few minutes later, he sped through town and hit the county road that led to the ranch.

He reached his destination just as the first rays of sunlight topped the surrounding trees. His boots started to smoke as he strode toward the house. Heat sizzled through the soles of his feet and sent spurts of pain up his calves.

He hit the front porch and stumbled inside. While he was out of the direct sunlight, there was still light filtering in through the windows, sucking at his strength as he wobbled toward the back hallway and the door that led to the wine cellar. He fumbled for the handle, tugged open the door and fell down the first few steps. The wood creaked shut behind him and the darkness quickly swallowed him up. He found his footing and took the steps two at a time until he reached the bottom of the staircase and another hallway.

Garret had spent an entire month breaking the cellar down into two large living areas. A single hallway divided the two sections. The door to the left was shut solid. A powerful presence emanated from inside and Dillon knew Garret had been wise enough to get his ass in bed at a decent hour.

Dillon reached for the second doorknob. A few seconds later, he yanked off his smoldering boots, stretched out the king-size bed that sat in one corner of the massive room and tried to calm his rapidly beating heart.

In the two months since he'd turned, he'd never stayed out past daybreak. He knew better. He closed his eyes and tried to welcome the all-encompassing blackness, but he was too worked up.

Not because he'd nearly gotten himself roasted.

Rather than the sharp odor of melted rubber and blistered skin, he smelled the intoxicating aroma of sweet wine and warm, aroused woman.

His nostrils flared and the scent magnified, along with the image of Meg, her body flushed and panting and eager for more.

Bobby's record didn't stand a chance in hell.

IT HAD BEEN THE MOST incredible sex *ever*.

That is, it would have been the most incredible sex *if* it had been real.

That's what Meg told herself when she opened her eyes the next morning, her T-shirt still bunched up under her arms, her undies laying next to her feet. Sunlight streamed through the open French doors, illuminating the stained sheets and empty wine bottle.

Heat rushed to her cheeks as she forced herself upright. She set the bottle on the nightstand, tossed the leftover Twinkie wrappers into a nearby trash can and tried to ignore the telltale ache between her legs as she climbed from the bed. She had nothing to be embarrassed about. She'd masturbated dozens of times before.

But never with Dillon Cash watching her.

A *fantasy* Dillon, she reminded herself as she headed for the bathroom and a cold shower. While last night's orgasm had been very real, the circumstances surrounding it had been anything but.

Dillon had *not* been standing in her doorway.

The wine bottle had *not* moved on its own.

N-o-t.

Her mind made up, she spent the next half hour getting ready for work.

When she finally walked out her front door, coffee in hand,

she'd managed to dismiss all of her crazy thoughts and face the truth—she was horny. So much so, that she was cooking up hot, sizzling fantasies and trying to turn them into reality.

She tossed her briefcase onto the passenger's seat, set her mug in the cup holder and turned to retrieve the newspaper that sat near the curb.

She didn't have time to waste entertaining the impossible. She had a business to run. She had a new ad running today, complete with a coupon, and she hoped with all of her heart that Glenda, the owner of Skull Creek's one and only newspaper, had gotten it right. Last time Meg had wanted to run a twenty-percent-off coupon, Glenda—who was seventy-six and extremely hard of hearing—had printed it as sixty. Meg had felt obliged to honor the coupon rather than piss off any customers, and so she'd lost a ton of money.

Instead of calling in the ad this time, she'd typed it out and handed it to the old woman herself.

She leaned over and reached for the paper. Just an inch shy, her gaze snagged on the black marks near the curb.

Her memory stirred and suddenly she was back in her bed, her breathing ragged and her body convulsing. Through the pleasure beating at her temples and the pounding of her heart, she heard the grumble of an engine and the squeal of tires and—

She abandoned the crazy thought, ignored the strange tingling in her gut and grabbed her newspaper. Climbing into her car, she shoved the key into the ignition and backed out. Shifting into Drive, she hit the gas and didn't look back.

Not even a peek.

Because no way in hell, heaven or the in-between had Dillon Cash shown up at her house last night, climbed onto her balcony and watched her have the best orgasm of her entire life.

At least that's what Meg told herself.

The trouble was, deep down, she wasn't so sure she believed it.

7

"GET. *OUT*."

The incredulous voice slid into Meg's ears. She glanced from her computer screen to the young woman who sat at a small table in the far corner of the stockroom, a newspaper spread out in front of her.

Terry Lynn Hargrove was Meg's one and only full-time employee. Unlike Meg's three part-time employees, she wasn't a local. She'd been born and raised in nearby Junction. They'd met nearly ten years ago at a community college in San Antonio when they'd both been fashion merchandising majors. Meg had gone on to graduate from SACC while Terry had quit to marry the man of her dreams.

Said man was now her ex-husband and the star of her revenge fantasies—she'd caught him cheating. Terry now lived in Skull Creek, worked for Meg during the day and went to school via several online study courses at night.

She had long brown hair, a centerfold figure, perfect teeth and brown eyes so wide and innocent they would make Bambi envious. She could also spot a couture knockoff at fifty paces. She wore the latest wraparound skirt with rhinestone rocker tee and knee-high cowboy boots. Back in Junction, she'd been Junction High's Best-Dressed Senior, as well as head cheerleader and homecoming queen. Last year, she'd earned the honor of being the first out-of-towner to make Tilly's coveted list. A huge honor she'd celebrated by going an extra five miles on her treadmill.

Terry was also a serious health nut since she'd packed on a

whopping twenty pounds while married to The Loser. She'd lost the weight along with the man, and was now determined to steer clear of both.

She sipped a soy protein shake and held up the newspaper. "Did you see this?"

"What?"

"The picture on the front page of last week's Lifestyle section?" Terry waved several sheets of newsprint.

"I haven't had time." Meg turned her attention back to the computer and finished ordering the prom dresses for the Weatherby twins—they'd settled on floor-length, bubblegum colored taffeta with rhinestones. A fitting that had gone surprisingly fast since the girls had come prepared with a copy of teen *Vogue* and a clear idea of what they wanted. "Why are we reading last week's paper?" she asked Terry.

"To catch up on the soaps. I'm here all day, so I don't get a chance to watch my favorites anymore, and I had a lot of homework last week so I couldn't read Marge's Titillating TV column. Claire told Darius she was pregnant."

"And Darius is…?"

"Only the hottest hunk on daytime TV. Claire says it's his, but she's a skank. I bet it's Juan's."

"Why don't you just record the shows?"

"Because then I would have to buy a DVD player that's made in China. I refuse to support an industry that's neck-deep in child labor."

Terry was also a humanitarian, a member of PETA and just last year she'd participated in a walk to free the lobsters.

"You could always get Tivo."

"And contribute to corporate world domination?"

"You can record multiple shows."

She seemed to think about it. "I *could* write an explicit letter of disapproval when I sign up. Just to make my position clear. Then it wouldn't be as if I were compromising my principles."

"Just bending them a little."

"Exactly." Terry's attention shifted back to the newspaper and she shook her head. "Dillon Cash and Ava Laraby. Can you believe that?"

Meg's fingers stalled on the keyboard. Obviously she wasn't the only one who hadn't bought his startling transformation.

She remembered last night and awareness rippled through her.

You bought it, sister, and it's just a matter of time until you're falling all over him just like every other woman in town.

She ignored the sudden zing of excitement that spiraled through her and summoned her initial disbelief. "It is pretty wild, isn't it?" Ava Laraby had been the dance captain for the Skull Creek Stars way back when. She'd been beautiful and outgoing and Dillon would have sold his soul to the devil for even a smile from her. "Not that people can't change," she heard herself add. "They most definitely can and we shouldn't be so judgmental."

"I'll try, but it just isn't that easy. I mean, *Dillon* and *Ava*. They don't blend. They're like water and oil. Fish and red wine. Gucci and Donna Karan."

"I wouldn't say they're so different. Dillon's not that far out of her league."

"Are you kidding?" She gave Meg a *get real* look. "*She's* way out of *his*. Her hotness has definitely fizzled even since I've known her. Look at that outfit? There's a reason they call them skinny jeans. They're for skinny people, otherwise they make your ass look like a billboard and I speak from experience." She took another drink of her shake. "And that shirt. Somebody needs to tell this girl that floral is over." She squinted. "And is that a spiral perm? Do they even do those anymore?"

"I happen to know for a fact that To Dye For does at least five spirals a month." When Terry arched an eyebrow, Meg shrugged. "Nikki mentioned it the last time I was in. She said it's still one of her hottest dos."

"Yeah, for the middle-aged mom's club." Terry shook her head. "They're opposite sides of the spectrum."

"You honestly think Dillon is too hot for Ava?"

Terry nailed her with a pointed stare. "You don't?" She tossed the paper.

Meg caught the newsprint and stared at the picture taken a few weeks ago at one of the local honky tonks. Even in worn Levi's and his *Computers Need Love Too* T-shirt, Dillon looked hot. Intense. Sexy. His hair was mussed, his jaw shadowed with stubble. His eyes glittered with a knowing sparkle that made her insides quiver.

"He looks even yummier in person," Terry continued. "I saw him over at Jimmy Jo's sports bar a few weeks back. I thought I was going to hyperventilate. But then I don't have to tell you that. You two are friends, right?"

"We don't see each other as often as we used to, but yes, we still talk."

Among other things, a tiny voice whispered. A voice Meg quickly stifled.

Terry grinned. "Maybe you could introduce us."

"I've already introduced you about a dozen times." But Terry had never given Dillon a second glance.

Until now.

Meg tossed the paper back and the girl grinned.

"My bad." She stared at the picture again. "I honestly don't remember him looking like this. He's definitely upped his hotness level. Has he been taking that Carnal class with you?"

"He's doing research online."

"On how to be a hottie?"

"Something like that."

"It's working."

Unfortunately.

Meg ignored the crazy thought. Dillon's newfound sex appeal was a good thing, even if it tested her control.

Because it tested her control.

If he could make her forget the man he'd been and inspire a megadose of lust for the man he'd become, then he could teach her how to do the same. Starting today. She'd already left two messages about lunch. Once he called her back, they would meet and the lessons would begin. Her next sexual encounter was sure to involve a man actually coming on to her, rather than the other way around.

That is, if she didn't backslide, forget her principles and hump Dillon first.

Her nipples tingled at the thought and she frowned. "Speaking of work—" she hit the Place Order button and pushed to her feet "—Elise and her daughter should be here any minute."

As if on cue, the bell on the front door tingled.

Terry sighed and set the paper aside. "Any ideas what you want me to set up in the dressing room?" she asked as she got to her feet.

"I don't think we need to get too complicated. All of Elise's girls went for the first Marc Jacobs I showed them."

"Marc Jacobs it is." Terry grinned. "The girl would have to be nuts to break that tradition."

Nuts, or just plain stubborn.

Meg came to that conclusion after a fruitless half hour with Elise's daughter, Honey Harwell.

She eyed the seventeen-year-old who stood on a platform in the monstrous dressing room. Honey had the same shade of blond hair as her mother and her four older sisters. But unlike the other Harwell women, Honey didn't wear her silky locks styled in the latest trend. Rather, she'd stuffed them under a baseball cap that read Lady Bulldogs in honor of the local girl's volleyball team. She wore blue jean overalls, a baseball jersey and tennis shoes.

"But your sister wore a dress just like this when she went to her prom," Elise Harwell told her youngest daughter. A former local beauty queen, the forty-something woman was now the mayor's wife and mother of five. As usual, her long blond hair was perfectly coiffed, her nails buffed and polished, and her face made-up with the latest Chanel lipstick and Christian Dior eye shadow. She wore a cream-colored silk blouse, matching skirt, a pair of gold sling-back stilettos and a determined look that said she wasn't leaving without a dress. "You simply *have* to go with this. It's too fabulous for words."

Honey eyed the dress her mother held up and shook her head. "No."

"But this is perfect," Elise insisted.

"It's *yellow*."

"Buttercup, dear—" the older woman waved a hand "—and it's the ideal shade for your skin tone. Just try it."

Honey shook her head and crossed her arms. "I'm not wearing anything named after a flower. Or anything that has flowers on it. Or anything that looks flouncy. I'm *so* not doing flouncy."

"But—"

"*No.*"

The woman looked ready to argue, but then her lips tightened. "All right, then. No flowers," she finally muttered. She let out an exasperated sigh as she handed the dress back to Meg. "And no flounce."

Bye-bye Marc.

"Of course." Meg slid the hanger onto a nearby peg and reached for a soft, shimmering pink number that hung on a nearby rack with several others Terry had brought in after Honey's first *"Not in this lifetime."* "I bet this would look great."

The girl took one look and pursed her lips. "If I wanted to look like a giant piece of bubble gum."

O-kay.

"If I didn't know better—" Elise forced a smile despite her pinched brow "—I'd say someone isn't even remotely excited about going to her one and only senior prom."

"I'm not excited about going. I don't want to go. You're making me."

"Nonsense." The woman waved red-tipped fingers. "Everyone goes to their senior prom. Why, every one of your sisters was either prom queen or a member of the royal court."

"I'm not my sisters, and I'm not going to be part of a royal anything. Talk about lame."

"There's nothing lame about being popular, dear," Elise said with tight lips, the flush creeping higher, all the way into her cheeks. "What about forest green? To match her eyes?" she asked Meg.

"Forget it," the girl said before Meg could reach for another selection. "I'm not going as a cucumber."

Elise's smile slipped. "Perhaps we could try something in red?"

"I'll look a Fruit Roll-Ups."

"How about salmon?"

The girl rolled her eyes. "That's just a fancy name for orange. I'm *so* not doing orange."

The woman's flushed cheeks turned splotchy. "How about navy blue?" she questioned.

"Too dark," Honey chimed in.

"How about bronze?"

"Too flashy."

"How about chartreuse?"

"Too Shrek-ey."

"How about a valium?"

Meg smiled. "I'm afraid I haven't restocked my supply of prescription sedatives, but I do have a nice Chardonnay chilling in the back."

"Thank God." Elise waved a hand. "I swear this child is going to send me to an early grave."

"We don't have to do this," Honey reminded her mother.

"Yes, we do. You can't miss your senior prom."

"Why not?"

"Because," Elise countered. "It's a once in a lifetime thing. A tradition. No daughter of mine is *not* going to her one and only senior prom. You'll regret it."

"I will not."

"Will, too."

Both Elise and her daughter stared at Meg. "Tell her," Elise said. "She'll regret it."

"Tell her I won't."

"I hate to say it, but you probably will."

Honey shrugged a stubborn shoulder. "You're just taking her side because you want to sell us a dress."

Meg opened her mouth to tell Honey that she didn't just want to sell a dress—she knew the regret firsthand—but Elise cut her off. "Honey Helen Harwell, that's a very unladylike thing to say. Just wait until I tell your father. You'll be lucky if he doesn't ground you."

Honey gave her first smile of the day. "Maybe he'll do it on prom night."

"Oh, no you don't. Don't think you're getting out of it that easy—"

"One glass of chilled Chardonnay coming right up," Meg cut in. "Why don't you two come up with a few must-haves—cut, color, style, etc—and when I get back I'll see what I can do to find something that makes everyone happy?" Elise nodded, Honey shrugged and Meg decided to get the hell out of Dodge before things turned physical between the former Miss Skull Creek and the captain of the Lady Bulldogs.

"Let's start over," Elise let out an exasperated sigh as she turned toward her daughter. "What color did *you* have in mind?"

"I don't know. Maybe camouflage."

"Forget the glass," Elise's voice caught up with Meg just before she disappeared through the curtained doorway. "Just bring me the whole damned bottle."

HE WAS THE HOTTEST GUY in the Piggly Wiggly.

Meg came to that conclusion later that afternoon as she stared at the tall dark haired stranger who stood in the meat section next to a life-size cutout of Roger the Rump Roast.

A white dress shirt, undone at the collar, framed his broad shoulders. Black trousers accented long legs, a trim waist and a really tight butt.

The guy, not Roger.

He leaned over to pick up a boneless shoulder roast. His trousers pulled and tugged in all the right places and Meg's mouth went dry. Her grip on the box of Twinkies she'd been holding loosened and thudded into her shopping cart. Last night's fantasy must still be affecting her.

She'd closed up shop over a half hour ago, after a long, endless day waiting for Dillon to return her phone calls.

Obviously he wasn't all that interested in her proposition, despite his claim otherwise.

And why would he be? He was already smoking hot. Wardrobe tips were just the icing on the already scrumptious cake.

Meanwhile she hadn't even made it into the oven.

If Dillon wasn't going to share his secret, then all hope of making Tilly's list was shot to hell and back. She was back at square one, still looking for that extra something that would give her an edge and force the men in town to see her in a different light.

A sexy light.

Sexually frustrated or not, she wasn't breaking her vow—no more first moves. No, if Dillon wasn't going to help her, she was doomed to wait until she found that extra something herself, which meant she was in store for more frustrating nights like the last one.

Which meant she needed Twinkies. Lots of Twinkies.

Hence her impromptu visit to the nearest grocery store.

She eyed the man again, doing a sweep once, twice, before shifting her attention to old man Darlington who stood near the frozen chickens, eyeing a package of chicken wings. Moving on, she spotted Hubert Humsucker stockpiling chocolate Ho Hos just a few feet away and Leonard Bunker who stood near an end cap checking out a Spam display.

Yes, he was definitely the hottest guy to make it past the open hoofs at the front entrance. Sure, he wasn't as super sexy as the star of last night's fantasy, but he was close.

An image stirred and she saw Dillon looking dark and delicious in faded jeans, a worn T-shirt and an expression that said he wanted to swallow her whole.

Okay, maybe hot guy wasn't *that* close. But he definitely beat out the handful of losers from her past. He was handsome enough. He was also new in town—the cousin of a cousin of a cousin of Shirley Waltrip who owned a local real estate firm. She had hired him straight out of broker school—which meant he had no preconceived notions about Meg. And, more importantly, he was smiling at her.

He was smiling at *her*.

She tamped down the urge to waltz over and introduce herself. Instead, she waited, maintaining eye contact, mentally urging him to come to her.

He abandoned the roast and stepped toward her. *Atta boy.* Her heart kicked up a notch, but it wasn't anywhere close to the breakneck stampede she'd felt last night.

Not that she was making comparisons. Last night had been so far out there. A wild and crazy dream.

This was the real thing.

He stepped closer, his strong, purposeful stride eating up the distance between them and she started to think that maybe she didn't need Dillon's secret, after all. Really, she'd been walking the walk and talking the talk for twelve years. It only made sense that some man would finally notice on his own.

She smiled and said, "Hi."

He smiled and said—

"Game three of the NBA finals. Spurs or the Heat?" she heard a voice say behind her.

Meg's head whipped around and she found herself staring at a short, squatty woman in her fifties. The lady wore a hair net, a white smock and a badge that read *Fiber is my Friend.*

Genevieve Crandall was one of the store's clerks. She worked the register and handled the incontinent section, which had grown to take up a complete aisle since the second retirement community had opened up on the outskirts of town just last month.

"The employees got a pool going with some of our steady customers," she told Meg. "Most everybody's putting their money on San Antonio, including Paul in cleaning products, on account of it's the closest thing we got to a home team. But Darlene in dairy likes the Heat because she has a sister down in Florida. Loretta and Lettie, the Bakersfield sisters who buy all the pork-'n-beans every time we run a special, put their money on Florida, too, 'cause they got a thing for that *CSI Miami* show. I like the show, but I ain't sure it's worth risking fifty bucks. I thought you could give me your pick."

"I'm sorry, Genevieve. I was talking to this nice gentleman." Meg shifted her attention back to hot guy. "I'm Meg. It's nice to meet you."

"Colt Grainger. I buy and sell ranch property."

"Shirley's cousin, right?"

"Twice removed, but yeah. I'm new around here and I could really use someone to show me around. I was wondering—"

"So was I," Genevieve persisted. "Come on, Meg. You gotta help an old lady out. I've got a new pair of orthopedic inserts riding on this. The Spurs have a better rebound record, but the Heat had multiple three-pointers last year. Both teams are neck and neck on blocked shots." She stared expectantly at Meg who stared expectantly at Colt.

A strange look came over his face as he eyed her. "You know basketball?"

"I—" Meg blurted, but it was Genevieve's crackly voice that chimed in, "Sure as shootin' she does. Why, this gal knows everything when it comes to sports. Girl was born to it. Daddy coached football over at the high school and took us to five consecutive championships. Four for our basketball team. Six for soccer. Eight track-and-field state finals. There ain't nothing Meg, here, don't know when it comes to sports. The girl's a legend around here." Her gaze swiveled to Meg. "Come on, sugar, who's your favorite?" Genevieve persisted.

"I think this gentleman got here first." Meg's gaze met hot guy's. "I think you were about to ask me something…?"

He looked puzzled for a split second before a thought seemed to strike. "Actually, I did."

Her heart paused and the air lodged. This was it. This guy

wanted her. She knew it. From the first moment he'd abandoned his roast, up until now. She read the sudden determination that leapt into his expression. The eagerness that blazed in his gaze. The strange way he looked at her now, as if he'd found the woman of his most erotic dreams.

"Yes?" Meg prodded.

"Spurs or Heat?" he blurted.

Meg blinked. "Excuse me?"

He shrugged and glanced at Genevieve. "I'd like to get in on the action if it's not too late."

"No problem," the old woman told him. "Fifty bucks and you're in."

So much for flying solo.

Meg spent the next few minutes giving her opinion on the upcoming game—it wasn't like she couldn't *not* help Genevieve, particularly when the woman offered to throw in a case of Twinkies at cost—and then turned on her heel and went in search of Dillon Cash.

They didn't call her Manhandler Meg for nothing.

8

"THERE'S A WOMAN IN TOWN looking for you." Nikki, Jake's girl-friend, made the announcement that evening when she opened the door to the small office where Dillon sat taking notes on the computer screen that blazed in front of him. He'd been at his terminal for an hour now, since sunset to be exact, and he had no intention of powering off anytime soon.

He was finally onto something.

Even more, he was now sufficiently distracted from the damned hunger that had gnawed away at him all day. The more he'd tried to sleep, the more he'd thought about Meg. He'd been so worked up by the time he'd rolled out of bed, that he'd needed to kill some time and cool off before he saw her again. He'd needed something mundane and boring, and so he'd headed to work.

But when he'd logged on to his blog—after perfecting the last line of code for his new software program—he'd gotten a shock that had juiced him up almost as much as the thought of Meg's sweet, succulent body.

Listed among the *Do me, baby* and *Let's be butt buddy* comments were four posts that actually detailed turning experiences similar to Garret's—the same sweet scent and the same medallion. All four were recent experiences and one even listed an actual name—Joe—and a location, Bryan Street, south side of Chicago, approximately six months ago.

It seemed that Joe had taken a bite out of IttyBittyVamp while he'd been club-hopping down in Chi town. In between clubs, Itty had run out of gas and had elected to knock on some poor sap's door to ask to use the phone, since he'd had a cheap cell phone and zero service.

Joe had given Itty a helluva lot more than a call to Triple AAA.

The newbie vamp was still screwed up over the sudden change, still trying to figure things out and deal with what was happening to him, and so he couldn't remember Joe's actual address. He just remembered waking up a block or so from the last club he'd gone to. He'd been bloody and alone and clueless as to what had just happened to him.

But he knew now and he was frantically trying to find a way to reverse the situation.

Dillon had given him the basic lowdown—destroy the source in order to free himself—and then he'd spent the hours afterward cyber-searching Joes in and around the area where Itty had opened his eyes for the first time as a vamp.

He'd come up with four of them.

"She's been asking around for you all day today," Nikki persisted, pulling Dillon from his thoughts and the computer screen.

He glanced up at the attractive blonde who stood in the doorway and shrugged. "What can I say? When you've got it, you've got it."

"Obviously." She grinned. "Candy Morgan—that waitress from the Shade Tree—talked nonstop about you last week. I think she wants seconds. And so does Lorelie Hellman and Gina Berkowitz and Tammy Fitzpatrick."

He shook his head. "As much as I'd like to oblige them all, Garret would have my head." That, and he couldn't actually remember any of those women. While he knew they'd been good—warm and sweet and sustaining—the only woman who lingered in his thoughts was Meg.

She was his biggest challenge, after all. So it only made sense she would get under his skin and stick in his brain.

That, or he actually *liked* her.

He shook away the thought and focused on Nikki. "So who was this woman?"

"Nobody I knew." Her expression grew serious. "When she

came into To Dye For, I thought she wanted a haircut. She sure as hell needed one what with all the split ends. But before I could get her in the chair, she started drilling me about you. How did I know you? When was the last time I'd seen you? What time did you open up shop? I told her you were on vacation and the shop was closed, but she didn't look like she bought it. I didn't think she would. I heard from Mary Lou Winegarten that she was at Pam's Pamper Park asking all sorts of questions, too. Knowing Pam, the woman probably got an earful about you being the new town stud." She shook her head. "But I'm a little worried. She seemed *too* anxious." Just as Nikki said the words, Jake appeared in the doorway behind her.

"Sounds like a vampire hunter to me," Jake offered, sliding his arms around Nikki's waist.

"Maybe." Nikki eyeballed the computer. "Whoever she is, I get the feeling that she's connected with your blog somehow."

"Why's that?"

"Because she referred to you as BigTexasVamp. She tried to cover up the slip, but I wasn't the only one who heard it. Charlie was doing highlights next to me and he thought she was talking about that new topless joint over in Tarpley—the one that features those dancers with the beehive hairdos who call themselves Big Texas Vampers. That's your screen name, right?"

Dillon nodded, his mind racing to find a connection between one of the posts and someone actually seeking him out. Sure, he'd had half a dozen women want to hook up with him, but to travel hundreds of miles just for sex?

As outrageous as it seemed, Dillon had watched enough Dr. Phil back in his human days—he'd always had the TV on while doing repairs at his shop—to know that there were desperate individuals willing to do just about anything to get laid.

"She came in during the day," Jake remarked. "So that means she's definitely human. She's either a vampire hunter, someone desperate to be turned, or maybe a groupie from another town who's heard about you and wants to see for herself."

Or maybe, just maybe, she had something to do with the Ancient One.

Dillon wasn't sure where the thought came from, except that it seemed too coincidental that the very day he received a concrete lead, a strange woman showed up in town looking for him.

"Regardless, you should watch your back," Jake told him, concern evident on the older vampire's face. "Garret and I are going to look around and see what we can find out about her. In the meantime, do what you can to lay low and avoid a confrontation."

"I can take care of myself."

"I know that, but there's no reason to prove it. Just be careful." He gathered Nikki closer, his arms tightening as if he never meant to let her go.

He didn't. He was crazy about her and she was equally crazy about him, despite the fact that she was still human.

Because of it, a voice in his head whispered.

Jake was a vampire and so any woman he took a fancy to would want him more than her next breath.

At the same time, there was something about the way Nikki looked at Jake that went beyond wanting to rip his clothes off and have wild and crazy sex. She wanted *him,* the man he'd been and the vampire he'd become. The whole package.

A pang of envy shot through Dillon as he watched the couple disappear out into the fabrication shop where Garret was busy welding the handlebars for his latest creation.

Not because he wanted anyone—especially Meg—to feel the same unconditional love for him. To feel love, period.

Sure, he liked Meg. But the last thing—the very *last* thing— Dillon wanted was for any woman to fall in love with him, and vice versa. He didn't need a relationship right now. He had a record to break and if the sudden anxiety pumping through his veins was any indication—that and the gut feeling that he was really and truly on to something—his days as a vampire were numbered.

All the more reason to table his research for now and get the hell out of the shop. He stored his notes and powered off the computer. Pushing to his feet, he tapped on the glass, signaled goodbye to Garret, Jake and Nikki and headed out the back door.

He'd promised to give Meg a few sex lessons, and it was time to start her education.

WHEN MEG PULLED UP IN front of Dillon's house and killed the engine, the sun had already set and darkness blanketed the area. He lived on the outskirts of town, the nearest neighbor at least a half a block down the gravel road. Not a single light burned inside the sprawling one-story building.

She debated whether or not to get out of the car. He wasn't home. She already knew that. Just like he hadn't been at the computer shop. The place had been just as dark, a sign hanging in the front window that read Closed Temporarily for Renovations.

Right. And she had a dozen men falling all over themselves to be her personal sex slaves.

She'd peered through the window and, sure enough, there hadn't been a ladder or a nail gun in sight. She'd tried room four at the motel, too, but he'd already checked out.

Relief niggled at her. Not that she cared if he did the nasty with Miss Hot Chick again. It's just that she'd hoped—she'd prayed—that they could start their lessons right away. The fact that he wasn't shacked up at the inn for another night was definitely a sign that he might be free.

If she could find him.

Her brain told her to put the car in Reverse, back out and look elsewhere—Big Bubba's honky tonk, the Shade Tree bar and grill, the Dairy Freeze—anyplace, *every* place where members of the opposite sex met to mix and mingle in Skull Creek. They were all possibilities worthy of a quick look now that Dillon had turned into Mr. Hook Up. He sure as hell wouldn't be sitting at home all by his lonesome.

Still.

She killed the engine and climbed out of the front seat just to be sure.

Maybe he was taking a nap. After last night—correction, after the last two months—he had to be exhausted. She grasped at the hope, ignored the apprehension that wiggled down her spine and started for the door.

The gleam of her headlights sliced through the darkness, pushing back the shadows and giving her a blazing trail toward the wraparound porch. Awareness prickled the hairs on the back of her neck with each step.

She couldn't shake the sudden feeling that someone was watching her.

If only.

The sad truth? Dillon was most certainly out on yet another date. At that very moment he was probably smiling that sexy smile of his and whichever woman was the flavor of the night was undoubtedly ripping off her clothes.

Meanwhile, Meg was here. The soft ground sucking at her favorite stilettos. The darkness chasing goose bumps up and down her spine. A rope tightening around her ankles—

The thought slammed to a halt as she glanced down. Sure enough, she'd stepped into a roped circle spread out in the grass. The slack had tightened. The rope had hiked up around her ankles. Nylon cut into her tender flesh and—

"Now!"

The man's urgent voice cracked open the silence and before she could breathe, much less scream, her legs were jerked out from beneath her. One of her heels stuck in the ground and the ankle strap snapped. Her foot yanked free and she flipped. In the blink of an eye, she found herself dangling upside down from a massive oak tree in Dillon's front yard.

The blood rushed to her head and she blinked, her body flailing as a pair of shadows rushed at her. The next few moments seemed to pass in slow motion, the voices unreal yet oh, so familiar.

"You were supposed to wait for me," said shadow number one, the voice high-pitched and distinctly female.

"Sorry, dear." Shadow number two struggled with Meg's flailing arms.

"No sense crying now," came the female's voice. "Just get the handcuffs on him."

"Handcuffs? I don't have the handcuffs," said number two. "I gave you the handcuffs to wipe down with antibacterial wipes."

"And I wiped them and gave them back. I set them right on the table next to the LYSOL. Didn't you pick them up?"

"Uh, oh." Shadow number two released Meg, turned and high-tailed it around the house.

Number one plopped a hand on her hip and shook her head. "I swear that man would forget his name if it wasn't for me."

Meg blinked against the sudden pressure in her skull and forced her eyes to focus. She peered through the darkness at the upside down figure dressed in a black jogging suit. "Mrs. Cash?"

The shadow loomed closer and a familiar face came into view. "Meg? Dear, is that you?"

Relief rushed through Meg and washed away the fear that had gripped her. "Guilty."

"I got the handcuffs," came the winded voice of the man who trotted around the corner of the house. He was dressed in black also, but unlike Dora Cash, his face was obscured behind a ski mask. "I brought the stun gun, too." He waved the small hand-held device. "I figure we'll zap him and then do the handcuffs—"

"No!" Meg and Dora said in unison.

"But we'll never get the handcuffs on," the man protested.

"It's not Dillon," Dora told her husband. "It's Meg."

"Meg?" Harold Cash lifted his ski mask, pulled a pair of bifocals from his pants pocket and shoved them on. "Meg Sweeney?"

"Hey there, Mr. Cash." Meg wiggled her fingers. "I was just looking for Dillon."

"You and us both," Dora told her. "We've been camped out in his front yard for the past few weeks trying to catch him when he came home. But he never showed. So we decided to switch tactics and move our tent to the backyard, that way he might think we've given up and come back. I mean, he has to come home sometime, right?"

"You would think so."

"One of us has been here day in and day out—with the exception of those three ER visits—and we still haven't seen him," Harold said.

"Poor Harold, here, had this red boil come up on the back of his neck," Dora chimed in. "My aunt's husband's sister had that and it spread until his entire head was inflamed. It caused major brain damage. Luckily, Harold's wasn't that bad."

"It was just a mosquito bite," the man told his wife.

"There is no *just*. Mosquito bites are dangerous. People die from them all the time. That's why I bought the mosquito netting even though we invested in four bug lamps, a dozen citronella candles and a case of bug spray. You can't be too careful."

"The second visit was because of a paper cut I got opening the carton," Harold added.

"Staph is a serious thing," Dora said.

"And then I got indigestion from a can of chili."

"People mistake heart attacks for indigestion all the time. Besides, I told you not to eat that chili. Spicy food is bad for your intestines."

"So is Mace, but that didn't stop you from making me go after that group of ferocious Girl Scouts."

"How was I to know they were armed? They were Girl Scouts, for Pete's sake. Besides, I thought it was Dillon."

"There were four of them, dear."

"I thought it was Dillon and a few of his fellow cult members."

"They were all less than four feet tall."

"They could have amputated his legs to keep him from running away."

"They were pulling a wagon full of cookies."

"The wagon could have been for my poor legless baby." She shook her head. "It was an honest mistake that could have been prevented if you'd been wearing your glasses."

"I can't wear them with this mask."

"So leave the mask off."

"It goes with the suit. Besides, if it hadn't been for the mask, I would have gotten a face full of Mace. That would have been ER trip number four. Our insurance company would have dropped us on the spot."

"They can't do that. We have the ultra premium plus plan that even covers pre-existing—"

"Excuse me," Meg cut in. "I have the cheap value plan that doesn't pay for any ER visits, so can someone please cut me down before I start bleeding out of my eyeballs?"

"Why, yes. Of course, dear. Harold, where's your knife?"

"I don't have the knife. You borrowed the knife to open that mosquito netting."

"And then I gave it back."

"No, you didn't."

"I most certainly did—"

"Everything's getting blurry," Meg cut in.

The two scrambled around back.

A few minutes later, Dora Cash worked at the nylon with a large kitchen knife while Harold kept a steady hold on Meg to keep her from crashing to the ground. A few more seconds, a near death experience when Dora nicked her finger, and finally the rope snapped.

Harold helped Meg to her feet before turning to his wife who clutched her finger. "Should I call 911?"

"Don't be silly." She smiled. "It's not like I'm going to drop dead at any moment." Her expression faded into serious intent. "It takes at least a few hours for most bacterial infections to set in, which means we have more than enough time to make it to the E.R. over in Junction."

"Sorry about the misunderstanding," Dora told Meg as Harold went to get their car, which they'd parked down the street. "We didn't mean to ruin your shoe." She indicated the one high heel that was still stuck in the ground.

"It's okay." Meg pulled the shoe free, stared at the broken ankle strap and tried to tamp down a rush of disappointment.

A feeling that had nothing to do with her ruined footwear and everything to do with the hot, hunky man she couldn't get off her mind or out of her fantasies.

The house had been her last hope since she had no intention of barging into Big Bubba's and interrupting Dillon with another woman. Which meant she was heading home, to an empty house and a box of Twinkies. And maybe even her favorite sweatpants and her lucky Cowboys T-shirt, still packed away in a box in her upstairs closet.

Hey, if she was going to backslide, she might as well go all the way.

She shrugged. "I didn't have any special plans tonight anyway."

SHE MEANT TO GO HOME.

She even went so far as to pull into the driveway and open the car door. But then she spotted the telltale tread marks near the curb, and just like that, she slammed the door shut, gunned the engine and headed over to her shop.

The next two hours were spent getting a jump start on tomorrow's workload and trying not to think about Dillon and the fact that he'd obviously changed his mind about helping her.

Because she wasn't sexy enough.

The truth taunted her, eating away at her self-confidence as she re-arranged her front window displays and moved on to unpack the new shipment of merchandise stacked near the main counter. She sliced open the first box, pulled aside several layers of bubble wrap and unearthed the metallic dresses she'd ordered at the last trunk show in Austin.

Not that she cared. It wasn't about being sexy enough for Dillon. It was about appealing to the rest of the male population of Skull Creek. She could care less if Dillon would rather boink his way through the current Hot Chicks list than keep his word to his oldest and dearest friend.

She fought down a wave of self-pity and pulled a low-cut silver number from the box. She held the dress up against her and eyeballed her reflection in the mirrored wall behind the cash register.

Not bad, but somehow, it wasn't as great as she remembered.

A few seconds later, she peeled off her clothes in a nearby dressing room and let the material slither over her head. A few tugs and pulls and…there. She walked back out to the front and stared at her reflection.

That was more like it.

The hem hit her mid-thigh, the silver fabric molding to her legs and waist. The neckline was a plunging halter that accented her cleavage and outlined her full breasts. Everything about it screamed *Hello? Hot female here*.

Which was why she'd ordered it in the first place.

Why she ordered every item in her store.

It was all about embracing her womanhood. Reveling in it.

She eyed her reflection again. Mission accomplished. She couldn't look any more feminine.

Yet here she was. All alone.

"It's not about the dress."

At the sound of Dillon's deep voice, Meg's head snapped up. She saw him standing on the other side of the glass door.

He wore jeans and a plain white T-shirt. The soft cotton molded to his broad shoulders, the sleeves falling just shy of the slave band tattoos that encircled both biceps. His green eyes gleamed with an intensity that screamed *hold on to your panties*.

She had the fleeting thought that no way could she have heard his voice so clearly and distinctly with a wall of thick glass between them. But then he grinned and her heart kick-started, and all thought faded in a rush of desire so intense it made her legs tremble.

He motioned her to unlock the door.

She fought down the urge to strip naked, haul open the door and do a full body tackle. Drawing a deep, steadying breath, she took one step forward, then another. Calm. Controlled. Still, her heart beat a frantic rhythm. Just as her hands touched the key to throw the dead bolt, a wave of anxiety went through her, followed by a bolt of pure, unadulterated lust. Her breath caught. She hesitated and sent up a fervent prayer for divine intervention.

As hot and bothered as she was—and at nothing more than a glance—she knew she was going to need all the help she could get.

9

"WHAT ARE YOU DOING HERE?" Meg asked, pulling open the door.

"Our first lesson." Dillon's gaze collided with hers. "Don't tell me you forgot about it?"

"I thought you were the one who forgot. It's half past nine."

"I had a few things to do first." He indicated the brown grocery sacks that filled his muscular arms. "But I'm here now." He winked. "Armed and ready."

Her tummy fluttered with excitement. "You're really good."

"How's that?"

"You've got the flirting down perfect." She shook her head. "But you don't have to do it with me." *Please.* "I don't need an actual demonstration. I just need to know *how* you do it."

His teasing grin faded into a serious expression. His green gaze brightened. "Then let's get to it."

"What's all this?" she asked as he deposited both sacks onto the counter near her cash register.

"A few things—" he rummaged inside one of the bags and pulled out a small jar of cherries "—to whet your appetite."

"I'm not really hungry."

He grinned and gave her a smoldering look. "Not yet."

She fought down a wave of excitement as she watched him unpack. A can of whipped cream, a small box of chocolates, a six pack of individual pudding snacks, three different pints of ice cream, a can of diet soda, a bottle of sweet tea, some orange juice and a large slush. "You've been to the Quickie Mart out on the highway."

"The Piggly Wiggly had already closed and it was the only

place open this late." He set the bags behind the register and shoved a large, tanned hand into his pocket to unearth a red, white and blue bandana. His gaze collided with hers and his eyes gleamed a bright, vivid blue—

She blinked. Just like that, the color faded into a rich emerald green. Had she just imagined the strange color?

Duh. Of course you imagined it. He has green eyes, not blue. He's always had green eyes.

"School's in session," he said, his deep voice killing any more speculation as he circled and came up behind her. The hard wall of his chest kissed her shoulder blades. She caught a quick glimpse of them in the mirror behind the counter and her stomach hollowed out at the provocative picture they made. He looked so large and powerful and intense. And she looked so…*hungry.*

The realization struck as she noted her glittering eyes and parted lips, the way her body fairly trembled in anticipation.

Of course, she was trembling. She'd been waiting for this for a long, long time.

Since the ninth grade.

His heavily muscled arms grazed her bare shoulders, distracting her from the ridiculous thought. He settled the bandana over her eyes and blotted out the truth staring back at her. "I want you to forget everything else and focus on what I'm going to put into your mouth."

"And how is this going to help me convince the rest of the town that I'm sexy?"

"Being sexy isn't about what clothes you're wearing or what kind of sheets you have." His deep, husky voice reminded her of last night's dream and she felt her cheeks heat. "It's about being sensuous." Strong fingers brushed her temple, her cheekbone as he adjusted the bandana. "This little exercise is going to get you in touch with your sense of taste. After that, we'll move on to the other senses—touch, smell, sight, sound."

With her vision gone, her others senses became sharper in that next instant. Her nostrils flared with the aroma of warm, hunky male. Her skin prickled from the heat of his hands burning into her arms as he led her to the far edge of the rectangular countertop. He turned her until her back was to the end of the counter and then his hands went to her upper thighs.

When the realization hit, panic bolted through her, followed by an avalanche of excitement. Her breathing quickened. Her pulse pounded.

"What are you doing?" she blurted as he gripped the back of her thighs and lifted her.

"Making things more convenient."

She quickly found herself perched on the end of the long, rectangular countertop, the groceries spread out the length behind her. She could feel the coldness of one of the ice cream cartons seep through the thin material covering her right buttock. A freezing contrast to the heat of the male hands that slid down the outside of her upper legs, over her knees to the tender skin inside. He urged her legs apart and wedged himself between them. Worn denim grazed her inner thighs and awareness rushed through her. Her ears tingled at the deep, husky murmur of his voice.

"There. Now we've got plenty of room. You can lie back if you want."

Yeah, baby.

The notion rushed through her head and she stiffened. He was too close, too overwhelming and with her eyes covered, she experienced a rush of vulnerability she hadn't felt in a long, long time. Suddenly, she was back in high school, her insides tingling in anticipation of her first actual kiss.

A kiss that had been *the* worst of her entire life.

"I'd rather sit." She shifted, trying to find a comfortable position where they weren't actually touching. "You know, I really don't see why you can't just give me a copy of your online research," she said, eager to put some distance between them and kill the intimacy. She went for the blindfold. "I'm really better at studying than any actual hands-on training." Strong, warm hands caught hers before she could pull the material free.

"That's the point, isn't it? To get you out of your comfort zone? Obviously what you're doing isn't working. We need to try something new." He urged her hands back down to her sides. "Stop fighting and work with me, Meg. Otherwise, I'm going to think you like sitting home every Saturday night."

"I don't sit home *every* Saturday night. I go out once in a while." She swallowed. "Just not with hot guys."

His warm rumble of laughter slid into her eardrums. "This will change that. *If* you give it a chance." Before she could reply, she felt the press of something hard against her lips. "Now stop fighting and open up."

The scent of chocolate filled her nostrils and her stomach gave a traitorous grumble.

"The object of this exercise is for you to guess what I'm feeding you," he continued. "Focus on the flavor and texture." His voice, so rich and deep, stirred her even more than the sugary sweet decadence. "Take your time to savor every mouthful. Then tell me what you think."

And what you want.

The deep command echoed in her head, as if he'd whispered the words right into her ear.

He hadn't.

She hadn't felt the rush of his breath against her temple, the graze of his lips. Nothing. Just the crazy feeling that he'd somehow, someway, invaded her thoughts.

Wariness wiggled up her spine and she had the sudden urge to hop off the counter and make a run for it. But then her stomach grumbled again and her mouth seemed to open of its own accord.

She sank her teeth into the sweet confection he fed her and focused on the burst of flavor rather than the urge to drag her tongue across the tip of his finger and taste him instead.

"Let's see…" she said, savoring the delicious mouthful.

Chocolate melted on her tongue, stirring her nerves into a euphoric buzz. She chewed and did her best to ignore the massive man who loomed in front of her. So close she could touch him if she leaned forward just so…

If.

She balled her fists and tried to concentrate on the specific flavors overwhelming her taste buds. His large hands settled on the tops of her thighs as he waited and awareness prickled her skin. Her stomach quivered as she swallowed.

"It's, um—" she licked her lips and tried to differentiate the different flavors that lingered in her mouth and made it tingle "—milk chocolate with a darker, more rich chocolate inside. Fudge," she blurted, as the realization hit. "It's milk chocolate with a fudge center. I'd say…a truffle from that box of chocolates?"

"You might be a quick study, after all."

She smiled, but the expression died when she felt the cool pressure of something at the corner of her mouth. His fingers moved and the thing he was holding slid across her bottom lip, teasing and tantalizing, until she forgot all about talking and opened her mouth.

A few seconds later, she bit down on a ripe, succulent piece of fruit. Juice spurted, drenching the inside of her mouth and trickling from the corner. "Cherry," she said, as she tried to catch the drop with her tongue.

"Bingo." The word was deep and husky. If she hadn't known better, she would have sworn she felt the soft flutter of his lips at the corner of her mouth, the soft flick of his tongue—

The thought shattered as she snatched the blindfold down to find him looming in front of her, his face several inches away, his gaze hooked on her face.

He frowned. "What's wrong?"

"I just thought…" *That you were going to kiss me.* She shook her head. "Nothing. I just got a little claustrophobic."

"Since when are you claustrophobic?"

Since the hottest guy in town walked into her boutique, hiked her up onto the far end of the counter, stepped between her legs and started mucking up her common sense.

"Can we just get on with this?" She pulled the blindfold back into place. "Come on. Give me something else." She opened her mouth. Several seconds ticked by, but then she felt the edge of a foam cup. A mouthful of slushee slid past her lips and iced her tongue.

"Cherry," she murmured.

"This isn't part of the test." He chuckled. "It's just to wash everything down."

"I don't need a drink. I'm fine. Just get to the next thing."

"Be patient, sugar. We've got all night."

All night? No way could she make it fifteen more minutes without making a move, much less an entire night.

"I'm hungry," she blurted. "Famished. Starved. Hurry up." Her heart thundered in her ears as she sat, waiting for more.

Her ears prickled to the tear of cardboard, the soft *pop* as a lid pulled free. After what seemed like forever, she finally felt the press of plastic at her bottom lip. A heartbeat later, he spooned a mouthful of something soft and sweet and scrumptious into her mouth.

"Chocolate pudding," she murmured, concentrating on the sudden rush of *yummm* that spiraled through her, rather than the man responsible.

She felt the hard press of his thigh against the inside of her knee and her nipples pebbled. She licked her lips.

Another spoon and the flavor of cold cream cheese and graham crackers exploded on her tongue. "Cheesecake ice cream." Another mouthful and her insides tingled. "Mmm... strawberry this time."

"Maybe you don't need me."

"That, or you've lost the element of surprise. I saw you unpack the grocery sack, remember?"

"So you know what I'm going to feed you before you taste it?"

She nodded. "We've done everything except the whipped cream. So I know that's what I'll get to taste next."

"That, or maybe I'll do a little tasting of my own." She felt his body weight shift as he dropped to his knees.

"What's that supposed to—" The words faded into a sharp intake of breath as he touched his lips to the inside of her thigh.

"Mmm," he murmured against her bare skin. "Definitely sweet." The soft rumble stirred a tremor and she felt the sudden wetness between her legs.

"You really shouldn't be doing this." *Excuse me?* This was exactly what he should be doing. What she'd wanted him to do from the very beginning—to make the first move and ravish her.

He was ravishing, all right.

At the same time, when she'd pictured a man falling all over her, he'd usually started a little higher up.

Dillon wasn't anywhere close to hauling her into his arms and kissing her senseless. Not in the traditional sense, that is. Even more, there was nothing wild and uncontrollable about his actions. The hands that pressed against her thighs were too purposeful, the mouth nibbling at her too intent. As if he were in complete control with one objective in mind—to push her to the edge until she was the one who lost her wits.

Never.

That's what she told herself. What she fully intended to tell him.

But it had been so long since a man had touched her like this—forever, in fact—and she couldn't seem to find her voice.

Her few sexual encounters had always been brief and to the point, and she'd always been the one in the driver's seat. The one on her knees, pushing some man to the brink rather than the other way around.

Not this time.

Dillon nibbled and licked his way slowly—deliciously slow—toward the heart of her and anticipation bubbled. She tried to remember that they were in her boutique, in full view of anyone who happened by and looked through the glass storefront.

Rather than zapping some sense into her, the thought made her that much more excited.

Instead of resisting, she found herself opening her legs even wider, her body begging him closer, while her head was telling her to pull off the blindfold and put a stop to this before she sailed over the edge, straight into the land of *Give it to me baby, or else!*

She wouldn't. No matter how much he worked her up.

No way. No how. Uh, uh.

While she wasn't resisting, she wasn't going to take the lead and move a muscle.

Her mind made up, she braced herself as he trailed his tongue over the silk covering her wet heat and pushed the material into her slit until her flesh plumped on either side. He licked, stroking and stirring the sensitive flesh until she squirmed and shoved her fingers into his silky hair.

Okay, so she *had* to move.

But there was a big difference between holding on for the ride and jumping into the driver's seat.

At the same time, there seemed nothing wrong with being a little enthusiastic. It wasn't like she was begging for it. She was just giving him a little encouragement.

He gripped the edge of her panties and she lifted her hips to accommodate him. The lacey material slithered down her legs. He caught her ankles and urged her knees over his shoulders. Large hands slid beneath her buttocks as he drew her to the very edge of the counter. At his first long lick, the air bolted from her lungs.

His tongue parted her and he lapped at her sensitive clit. He tasted and savored, stroking, plunging, driving her mindless until her body wound so tight that she couldn't stand it anymore. A cry vibrated from her throat and shattered the stillness that surrounded them. Her orgasm gripped her and held tight for the next several seconds. Her body trembled and her insides convulsed. She barely resisted the urge to haul him to his feet and press her body against his.

Because as great as the feeling was, it just made her want to forget her inhibitions, peel his clothes off, push him down and climb on top.

And suddenly, with her own ragged breaths echoing in her

ears and her heart pumping furiously in her chest, that didn't seem like such a bad idea.

After all, he'd started it.

DILLON DRANK IN THE intoxicating taste of her. His hands kneaded her sweet ass, holding her close as her orgasm rippled through her. It wasn't the actual act of having sex with a woman that fed the beast that lived and breathed inside of him. It was her orgasm.

Her essence.

When a woman peaked, she pulsed with the sweetest, most potent, most sustaining energy.

Meg Sweeney was the sweetest yet.

The thought struck as he fit his lips more closely on her throbbing slit. Her body convulsed against his mouth and he drank from her, relishing the rush of heat. Her essence fed him all of five seconds. But instead of being satisfied, he felt even hungrier. Starving. The urge to push her back onto the counter and sink his cock into the decadent warmth gripped him and the beast took control.

He pushed to his feet, the tight bulge in his pants brushing against her sensitive flesh as he pushed closer, urging her legs wider, her back flat against the counter top. Candy bars sailed to the carpeted floor. The can of whipped cream upended, clattering on the counter and diving over the edge.

Tugging at his waistband, he unfastened the button and gripped the zipper. He was just about to shove the zipper down when her soft voice pushed past the roar in his ears.

"Wait. I want to see this."

Her hands went to the blindfold and his memory stirred. He remembered the excitement on her face when he'd leaned in for that first kiss so long ago. Followed by the disappointment when it was all said and done.

He stiffened as she pulled the bandana down and gazed up at him, a victorious light gleaming in her blue eyes. Her full lips curved into a smile and where he'd been about to pull away, suddenly he had half a mind to finish what he'd been fool enough to start.

He liked seeing her smile.

Things are different now.

You're different.

It was true. He wouldn't come anywhere close to disappointing her now the way he had back then. He *knew* it.

Still…

She was different. She had a strong will. Strong enough to resist him despite his vampire charisma. Which meant there was the smallest possibility that she might not think he was all that in the sack.

Not unless she was already out of her mind with lust.

So much that *she* reached out to *him*.

He stared down at her. She made an inviting picture, the metallic dress riding her waist, her legs spread wide, her ass bare on the glass countertop, her nipples hard, throbbing points beneath the skimpy material. Expectancy etched her beautiful features as she waited for him to free his cock and sink into her.

Hunger gripped him, twisting at his insides, shaking his already tentative control. He fought against the sensation and fixed his attention on her eyes. He could see the victory that pulsed through her.

The anticipation.

The *hell, yeah.*

"I think you're getting it, sugar," he said, his voice deep and raspy and raw. He slid his button back into place, planted a quick, rough kiss against her full lips, then turned on his heel and walked away.

Because no way was Dillon blowing his one chance to prove to himself that he wasn't the geek that everybody thought. He'd waited too long and battled too many doubts.

The next move was Meg's.

10

SHE COULDN'T MOVE A muscle.

Meg came to that conclusion as she stared up at the ceiling, her body still tingling from Dillon's delicious mouth. Even more, she didn't want to move. She wanted to lie there, to remember the feeling of his hands and his lips on her body. To bask in the tiny convulsions still clenching and unclenching inside of her. To revel in the knowledge that her dry spell had ended.

Sort of.

Reality struck and she tried to summon her disappointment that they hadn't actually had sex.

She should be upset.

She wasn't. Rather, she felt content.

And relieved.

As worked up as she'd been, she hadn't reached for him or pulled him close. She'd resisted the temptation and let him make all the moves.

Including that first kiss.

She swept her tongue over her bottom lip and tasted the wild ripeness of his mouth. A hungry spurt of desire went through her, followed by a burst of excitement.

He'd kissed *her.* A quick press of his lips that had been brief and to-the-point, and a hundred—no, make that a million—times better than the first.

Because he was different now. Bold. Confident. Sensual. *Sexy.*

And she was one lesson closer to following in his footsteps.

A smile curved her lips as she slid from the counter, retrieved her undies, and turned to clean up the mess they'd made. More than once, she caught herself tasting the leftovers, savoring them before she bagged them back up.

Sweet chocolate melted on her tongue.

Light, frothy whipped cream filled her mouth.

Fruity slush slithered down her throat.

The different tastes were highly stirring. The various textures extremely erotic.

By the time she'd put away the last of the supplies, her entire body felt alive. Aroused.

She shoved the bags into a nearby trash can and turned. Her gaze snagged on her reflection in the mirror and her breath caught.

This time she didn't notice the sexy cut of the metallic dress, but the woman beneath it. Her eyes appeared heavy-lidded, her cheeks flushed, her lips slick and red from the slush. She looked as if she'd just rolled out of bed after a night of wild lovemaking.

She looked desirable. *Sexy*.

Even more, she felt that way.

It was a feeling that stayed with her as she closed up shop and headed home to bed.

She didn't stop off for a quick Twinkie fix. She didn't bother putting on a pink nightshirt or a slinky nightie or even a skimpy thong.

For the first time, Meg Sweeney peeled off her clothes and crawled between the sheets wearing nothing but her own skin.

DILLON STARED AT THE woman behind the bar and noted the sway of her hips as she walked the few steps to the cooler, the way she positioned herself so that she could give him a bird's-eye view of her ample cleavage when she leaned down and reached for a chilled beer mug.

Her breasts jiggled and swayed as she set the mug on the counter and gripped the draft handle. Gold liquid streamed into the frosted glass and she licked her lips. Her nipples pressed decadently against the thin cotton of her tank top, *Grady's Bar & Grill* emblazoned across the front.

Either she was extremely thirsty and close to bursting at the thought of sucking down a cold one, or she wanted to suck something altogether different. One glimpse into her eyes—her thoughts—settled the controversy.

Libby Sue Wentmore. Early twenties. Bartending was just a way to pay the rent until she got her big break at the *American Idol* auditions and made it to Hollywood. From there it was a straight shot to the big time—from making the actual show and the final two, to a recording contract and an appearance at MTV's VMA awards, to her very own quarterback boyfriend. But she had her sights set on the hunk running the ball for the Packers rather than the Cowboys. Puh-lease. *Everybody* knew Green Bay kicked royal ass.

And speaking of ass…

She was more than willing to hand hers over to him.

"Here you go." She set the ice-cold draft down in front of him and gave him her most provocative smile. "Good for what ails you."

"Thanks." He lifted the mug and touched it to his lips.

Her gaze riveted on the motion and she licked her own lips.

"Is this your first time at Grady's?" she asked after he'd taken a long pull on the beer. "I don't think I've seen you around here before."

"First time." Dillon had driven over to Oyster Creek, a small town about a half hour north, on purpose. He'd been too worked up to go back to the bike shop. And much too hungry. He'd needed a woman.

One who wouldn't remind him of Meg, or Skull Creek, or the all-important fact that he still hadn't managed to break Bobby's record.

"I'm not from around here," he added.

"A tall, hunky stranger." She smiled again. "I like." Her expression faded into a look of pure hunger. "I get off in fifteen minutes. I could show you around if you're interested."

He tipped his mug toward her and took a long swig. "I'll meet you out back."

He spent the next ten minutes finishing his beer before he tossed several bills onto the counter and pushed to his feet. He cast one quick, hungry glance at the bartender who looked ready to hop up on the counter and take him on right there. She winked and he could practically feel her pulse beating against his lips, her lifeblood gushing into his mouth.

His groin tightened and his stomach grumbled and he turned just as one of the waitresses approached him.

"Hold up, buddy. This is yours." She held out a fresh beer.

"Sorry, but I didn't order another."

"Someone did." She pointed to the far end of the bar at a now vacant barstool. "That's funny. She was there just a second ago. Oh, well." She shrugged. "Enjoy."

He might have if he hadn't had the distinct feeling that something wasn't right. He felt it in the tightening of his chest and the tensing of his muscles. He drank in the faces that surrounded him and a barrage of thoughts rushed at him. He picked through fact after fact, searching for...

He wasn't sure. Something out of the ordinary maybe.

Or someone.

Most likely a groupie. At the same time, he couldn't dismiss the possibility of a vampire hunter. By blogging, he'd opened himself up to both.

He stiffened as a wave of anxiety washed through him. Followed by a burst of sheer desperation. Because as much as he knew it had to be one of the two, he couldn't shake the gut feeling that it was neither.

That whoever—whatever—was after him had something to do with the Ancient One himself.

"Let's get out of here." The bartender came up beside him. "Maybe pick up a pizza and head back to my place." She winked. "I'm starving."

The music and chaos seemed to fade, along with his speculation. Her pulse echoed a steady *ka-thunk, ka-thunk* in his head. His gut tightened and his gaze fixed on the smooth column of her throat. "You just read my mind, sugar."

"IT'S ABOUT TIME YOU showed up." Garret Sawyer sat at the kitchen table, a laptop open in front of him. He looked like a classic biker tonight with a black bandana tied around his head, a black Harley Davidson T-shirt and worn jeans. His feet were bare, his boots discarded a few feet away. "You're pushing it, don't you think?" He glanced at his watch. His arms flexed and bulged, accenting the telltale tattoos that encircled his biceps. "It's fifteen minutes until sunup."

"Plenty of time." Dillon collapsed in the chair directly across from Garret's.

"If you've got a hankering to deep fry your ass." Garret's attention shifted back to the laptop. He hit a few more keys before closing the lid and eyeballing Dillon. "You look like hell."

Garret had just fed.

Dillon could tell by the fierce gleam in the vampire's eyes, the flush of his cheeks and the sweet, sharp scent of blood that still clung to him.

His own stomach grumbled. "Thanks for the compliment."

Silence stretched between them as Garret continued to stare. "Have you been feeding?" he finally asked.

"I fed tonight."

"I'm talking blood, not sex." His eyes gleamed with a knowing light. "You're young. You need both right now."

Dillon knew that, which was why he'd taken the bartender back to her place. He could still see the tempting picture she'd made standing in the small living room, her eyes bright and determined and hungry.

She pulled her tank top over her head and bared her breasts. "Give it to me, baby," she said as she stepped toward him.

"Why don't you give it to me?" he countered as she pressed her body against his.

Her gaze collided with his and just like that, she knew what he wanted. Not consciously. But deep down she knew what he really wanted from her. What he needed.

She swept her hair aside and tilted her neck, offering him the sustenance he so desperately sought.

His groin tightened and his stomach clenched and he leaned forward...

And then he'd stopped.

Shit.

"You have to feed." Garret pushed to his feet and walked over to the refrigerator. He hauled open the door and retrieved a dark red plastic bag. He tossed it on the table. "You can't live on this stuff." The "stuff" referred to a limited supply of bagged blood Garret had managed to get his hands on when he'd paid a visit to an ex-girlfriend who worked a local blood bank. "It serves a purpose in a pinch—when you're trying to lay low or curb the hunger when it threatens to rage out of control—but it isn't a permanent fix." He snagged a beer from the fridge and picked up his laptop. "You'd do well to get used to what you are for now and just do it."

Dillon nodded. Not that he had a problem embracing his need for blood. He had no problems sinking his fangs into a warm, willing woman. It was just that he didn't want to. Not unless the warm, willing woman happened to be Meg.

Double shit.

"Don't fall for anyone," Garret told him. "I know Jake is hooked on Nikki, but he's the exception to the rule. The only exception. For the rest of us, it just doesn't work."

"It's not about a woman." It wasn't. He wasn't hung up on Meg herself, but what she stood for. She was the ultimate challenge and bedding her meant blazing a new trail as the town's studliest guy. End of story.

"Nikki told me about the woman."

Dillon nodded. "Jake thinks it's a groupie or a vampire hunter."

"More than likely."

"And the not so likely?"

"It's not worth considering," Garret said, but his expression wasn't half as convincing as his voice. "Just feed." He motioned to the bag. "Either way, you're going to need your strength." He turned and started for the hallway leading to the cellar.

"You feel it, don't you?"

Garret stalled in the doorway and turned. His body hummed with tension. "Feel what?"

"I don't know." Dillon shrugged. "It's like an awareness. Like something's close. Watching." His gaze collided with Garret's. "Maybe the Ancient One isn't as far away as we think. Maybe my blog is working and instead of locating him, he's located us."

"We should be so lucky." Garret shook his head. "I would know if he was here. Vampires can sense other vampires. You sense me, don't you? And Jake?"

Dillon nodded. Their presence was a constant in his mind. He could feel their power as distinctly as he could feel his own.

"It's instinctive and fierce," Garret went on. "Not subtle." He shook his head. "I'm sure whatever's bugging you is nothing." Even as he said the words, Dillon could tell Garret didn't believe it half as much as he wanted to. "I'm installing a security system here at the house. If she's a vampire hunter, she'll come after us during the day when we're most vulnerable. I don't think she's clued in to our location yet, otherwise she wouldn't still be asking so many questions."

"And if she's not a vampire hunter?"

Garret winked. "Then we can both stop worrying and have a good time."

Easier said than done.

The notion stayed with Dillon as he downed the blood and headed for the cellar. He kicked off his boots and stretched out on the bed, his gaze fixed on the ceiling.

But he didn't see the cedar beams crisscrossing the Sheetrock. He saw Meg spread out on the countertop, her body lush and inviting and damn near irresistible.

He tasted her, too, the ripe taste of wild, forbidden fruit still potent on his lips.

He smelled her—the faint scent of strawberries and chocolate and warm woman.

He heard her—the frantic beat of her heart and the long moan when she'd come apart against his mouth.

He even felt her—her sweet, round ass warming his palms, her frantic fingers tugging at his hair.

Deep in his gut, he knew he couldn't begin to drink from any other woman until he finished what he'd started with Meg. Until he seduced her to the point of no return, shattered Bobby's record and proved himself once and for all.

The sooner, the better.

"LOOKS LIKE SOMEONE'S been having ultra hot sex," Terry said when she walked in the back door of the boutique the next morning.

Meg stood near a rack pulling dresses for her first appointment. When Terry smiled and gave her a knowing look, a rush of heat swept from her toes to the roots of her hair.

"Dillon and I did not do the nasty."

Not yet.

Meg ignored her body's traitorous whisper and pulled an orchid chiffon dress from the mix. "Last night was strictly business," she went on. "I'm still flying solo in the orgasm department."

"Not you." Terry tossed her purse on a nearby shelf and headed for the small fridge that sat in the far corner. "I'm talking about me." She pulled a bottled yogurt from inside and popped the top. "Hank dropped by last night. One minute we were arguing over who was supposed to get the Tim McGraw CDs and the next, we were doing it on my kitchen table."

Meg's hand stalled just shy of a navy blue sheath. "But you hate Hank."

Terry shrugged. "An ex is like a large order of French fries. You know it's bad for you, but sometimes you just have to have one." She looked doubtful as she took a sip of her yogurt. "But it was just a one-night stand. It's not like we're moving in together and I'm back to binge eating Ben & Jerry's. I *so* can't do refined sugar anymore. Besides, I think Hank's an asshole. And he still thinks I'm a bitch." She smiled. "Which I am." She shook her head. "No, it was just a one-time thing. It's still over between us."

"Let's hope Hank thinks so," Meg added.

A frown pinched between Terry's eyebrows. "He knows." Her expression eased. "I like it." She indicated the rose colored taffeta Meg had just pulled from the rack. "Honey will go nuts."

"You bet she will." Meg ignored her own doubts about the Hank issue and let the woman change the subject. Meg wasn't exactly the voice of experience when it came to men. "These are the dresses she picked out of the magazines I gave her. Narrowing it down from this bunch should be no problem."

"True." Terry nodded. "But I'll get the wine just in case."

HONEY HATED THE DRESSES.

Which meant that two hours later, Meg was ready to pull her hair out and Elise had consumed an entire bottle of Chardonnay. The woman was now paying homage to the porcelain god in Meg's backroom while Honey played Astroturf Warriors on her hand-held Sony PSP.

"We need something to settle her stomach," Terry announced after checking on Elise for the tenth time. "Maybe I should head over to the grocery store."

"And leave me here to deal with Honey?" As if on cue, Honey let out a long string of cuss words with a few *illegal tackles* and *slow running backs* thrown into the mix. A moan from the restroom punctuated the tirade.

"You're the boss," Terry told Meg, "which means you take the bulk of responsibility when it comes to this place. Meaning, you get to wash Miss Filth's mouth out with soap *and* you get to wash the puke out of her mother's hair."

"Being the boss means I get to delegate that responsibility as

I see fit. And I definitely see you staying here while I head to the Piggly Wiggly."

"Bitch."

"Happy washing." Meg grinned and grabbed her purse. "I'll get Honey to look through the latest magazines and pick out something else. That should keep her quiet while I'm gone. Try giving Elise some coffee in the meantime. I'll be back in fifteen minutes."

"I really don't feel comfortable feeding someone something that's so addictive."

"If you'd rather take her home with you and let her sleep it off, be my guest."

"A little coffee never hurt anyone."

Five minutes later, Meg walked into the nearby grocery store. She picked up three different types of antacids and had just handed everything over to the cashier when she heard the deep voice behind her.

"I owe you big-time."

She handed over a twenty before turning to find Colt Grainger standing behind her. He wore black slacks, a white button-up dress shirt, the sleeves rolled up to his forearms and a big smile.

"Really? How's that?"

"I went with your pick for the play-off game and won a hundred bucks." He set a pack of disposable razors on the counter and reached for his wallet.

"Good for you." Meg ignored a rush of disappointment as she took the change the clerk handed her and stuffed it into her purse.

"You've really got an eye for sports." He handed over his money for the razors.

"Thanks." She grabbed her bag and started for the door.

"No, I mean it." He waved for the cashier to keep the change, snatched up his purchase and hurried after her. "Wait." He caught her hand just as she reached the sliding double doors. "I want to talk to you."

"The Spurs," she blurted, noting the curious stares of several cashiers and old Mr. Wickerby who was busy paying for a gallon of buttermilk. "The Spurs have the strongest turnover record and they throw more three-pointers than anyone else in the NBA. Both of those factors are weak for the other team."

"That's not what I wanted to talk to you about."

"It's not?"

"No. I mean, I guess it was, but then I saw you and you look…" His voice trailed off as he gave her a once-over. "Did you change your hair?"

She touched the blond locks, which she'd been wearing loose and long since senior year. "I washed it, but I do that every morning."

Another once-over. "You must be wearing different make-up."

"Just my usual pink passion lip gloss and sunrise blush."

"A new outfit?"

"They're all new to you," she reminded him. "We just met a few days ago."

He grinned, the expression fading as he studied her again. "I can't put my finger on it, but there's something different from the last time I saw you. You look…I don't know." He shook his head. "You just look really good, that's all."

Really *sexy*.

The truth whispered through her head and her heart gave a tiny kick. "Thanks."

"What do you say you and I go out Saturday night? I'd really like to take you to dinner. Maybe dancing."

"Really? Like a date?"

"That's what I was thinking."

A rush of happiness went through her. It was far from *"I have to lay you down and make made passionate love to you right now, or I'll go berserk,"* but it was a start.

She reveled in the feeling for a few seconds before she shook her head. "Actually, I already have plans." Dillon was basing his lessons on the five senses. One down, which meant she still had four to go before she would be ready to put her newly learned sensuality to the test. It was already Thursday and even if she and

Dillon met every night, they still wouldn't be finished in time. "What about next Friday?"

Hope flared in his gaze and he grinned. "That would work." He gave her another thorough once-over. "Are you sure you didn't so something different?"

She shook her head. "Just the same old, same old."

On the outside, but the inside…

Her mind rushed back to last night. She felt the slick glide of the cherry along her lips, tasted the burst of flavor, and her stomach hollowed out.

"It's really good seeing you again," he said, his voice deeper and his eyes brighter, as if he read the thoughts racing through her mind.

He didn't. At the same time, he saw the way such thoughts made her feel. He saw the woman she'd become rather than the tomboy she'd once been.

Thanks to Dillon.

"Next Friday," she said.

"Next Friday it is." He winked.

Meg waited for her stomach to pitch the way it did when Dillon winked at her.

The only thing she felt was a burst of satisfaction. The lessons were working! And she had the date to prove it.

Now if she could just hold it together and control herself for the last four lessons, she would be home free. Forget just asking her out. Colt Grainger, as well as every other available man in Skull Creek, would be falling all over her. She would be a shoe-in for Tilly's new list.

In the meantime…

Dillon's image pushed into her head and she remembered the way he'd looked the moment before he'd kissed her—his body taut, his face dark with passion, his eyes so deep and green and mesmerizing.

Not that she'd been the least bit mesmerized. She'd held her own last night and resisted temptation, and she would do the same tonight.

She was *not* jumping his bones and begging him to have sex with her.

No matter how much she suddenly wanted to.

SHE WOULD BE ALL OVER him tonight.

Guaranteed.

That's what Dillon told himself when he arrived at the boutique an hour after sunset. He'd hadn't even bothered to stop off at Skull Creek Choppers. Rather, he'd rolled out of bed, taken a shower, spent a half hour learning the ins and outs of Garret's new security system—complete with video surveillance and several different alarm codes—and then he'd headed straight here.

"Get your purse and let's go." He grabbed her hand and led her around the counter.

"But I've got some outfits to show you." She motioned to several boxes that sat stacked near the counter. "I had a few things overnighted—some shirts and jeans, a sports coat. Stuff you might look good in."

"Later. I want to show you something."

"I've seen it," she said when he pulled out the blindfold.

He grinned. "Not this." He folded the material and came up behind her to tie it into place.

"How can I see anything when my eyes are covered?"

"Sugar, you can see everything. Your mind will paint a clear picture based on the information it receives from your other senses."

"So sayeth the man without the blindfold."

"Just trust your instincts," he murmured.

Hair as soft as silk brushed his fingertips as he secured it at the back of her head. Before he could stop, he threaded his fingers through her hair and let the strands tease his palms. He leaned down and took a deep breath. The scent of strawberries filled his head and sent an echoing throb to his groin. His hand grazed the skin at the nape of her neck and her breath caught.

The sound, so soft and nearly discernable, vibrated in his eardrums and mesmerized him for a long moment. He tamped down on the lustful thoughts that swamped his senses and drew a deep, steadying breath. Not that he actually needed it, but he was still a new vampire and it was a habit he'd yet to break.

"Where are we going?" she asked as he took her hand and led her out to the curb where his bike was parked.

"You tell me." He helped her straddle the powerful machine, then turned to retrieve an extra helmet. "That's tonight's test. Based on what you hear and smell and feel, I want you to tell me where we're at."

She smiled. "We're standing in front of my shop."

"Not now, smart ass." He barely ignored the urge to capture her full lips and kiss her like he'd done last night. But slow this time. And thorough. "Once we get there." His fingertips brushed the underside of her chin and he felt the frantic thump of her pulse. A shudder ripped through him and his hands actually trembled.

Crazy. He was a vampire in complete and total control.

A hungry vampire who'd yet to feed on anything other than the bagged blood back at Garret's place.

He needed a real woman.

A warm woman.

This woman.

"Let's go." He straddled the bike in front of her in the hope that having her out of eyesight would ease the throbbing inside of him. It didn't. Her arms snaked around his waist. Her full breasts pressed against his shoulder blades. Her pelvis cradled his ass and her slender thighs framed his, and it was all he could do to turn the key on the bike and crank the friggin' engine.

As for driving... Thankfully, he didn't have to have steady hands for that.

He could let his mind take control and guide them.

Once they hit the back roads and headed outside of town, he did just that. He fixed his gaze on the moonlit road ahead and sent out the silent commands to the mass of metal beneath him.

Pick up the pace and get there already.

The engine roared and the bike gained speed. The tires ate up the dirt road at a furious pace, leaving a cloud of dust in their wake. While he still rested his hands on the handlebars, he wasn't the least bit concerned with steering.

No, the hands he kept in place to keep from touching her.

There would be plenty of time for that once they reached their destination.

11

"I'M REALLY NOT DRESSED for this," she yelled above the rush of wind.

Meg's skirt slid higher up her thighs, her crotch nestled firmly against Dillon's butt. The only thing between them was the thin cotton of her thong and his jeans, and it wasn't nearly enough at the frantic pace they were moving.

Not with the bumps and lurches and *ahhhhhh…*

His denim-clad butt rubbed deliciously between her legs and the sudden friction caused an avalanche of heat that doused her and cut off her oxygen supply for several long seconds. Pleasure speared her and she barely caught a moan before it sailed past her lips.

"What was that, sugar?"

"Nothing." It was bad enough she was getting turned on with little effort on his part. He was driving, for Pete's sake. Not paying her the least bit of attention. No flirty comments or smoldering looks or purposeful touches.

She blew out a deep breath. Jesus, she might as well just jump him right now.

Squelching the notion, she scooted as far back as she could on the seat and concentrated on keeping a scant inch between them. There. That was much better.

Except when they swayed, she slid from one side to the other. The leather rubbed against the backs of her thighs and she couldn't help but remember Dillon's hands gliding along her bare skin, cupping her bottom and pulling her closer—

Stop, already.

She stiffened and let the stinging wind whip some sense into her.

You don't want to have sex. You don't want to have sex. You don't want to have sex.

She recited the silent mantra and managed to distract herself all of five seconds before they veered to the right. The motorcycle hit a rut and jumped. She jerked on the seat, slid forward and just like that, she raced right back into the land of temptation.

She caught her bottom lip against a fierce burst of pleasure. She tangled her fingers in the soft cotton of his T-shirt, eager to keep her hands anchored in place at his waist. The last thing she needed was for him to know exactly how turned on she was.

While he'd made a few moves, he hadn't made *the* move— no whipping off his clothes and having sex with her. Which meant he didn't find her completely and totally irresistible.

Still, he had to be a little turned on, right?

She couldn't help but wonder. A curiosity that could be easily satisfied with a little southward gravitation of her hands. A few inches lower. A few strokes here. A few strokes there.

You don't want to have sex, remember? You don't want to have sex. You don't want to have sex. You don't.

Another bump and her body jumped. Her hands slipped. Her fingers grazed his crotch—accidentally, of course—and his spine went ramrod straight.

He was turned on, all right, and there was nothing little about it.

The knowledge stirred a burst of satisfaction that she wasn't alone in her desperation. At the same time, it made her that much more aware that she *wasn't alone in her desperation.*

Dillon wanted her, all right.

But enough to make the first move?

She felt the tautness of his muscled abs through the thin cotton of his shirt. Her nostrils flared and the scent of him—denim and fresh air and a wildness that stirred something deep and primal inside of her—slid into her head and skimmed across her senses. Stirring and rousing.

Another bump and she rubbed deliciously against him. Once. Twice.

By the time they skidded to a stop, Meg's entire body buzzed with awareness.

She hoped Dillon felt the same, but then he climbed from the bike and killed their connection, and she wasn't so sure. Even more, his voice was as smooth, as controlled as always and her hopes plummeted.

"We're here." He took both her hands, his fingers burning into her as he helped her get her footing. "Any ideas where we're at?"

She had ideas, all right.

Unfortunately, none involved their location.

She tried to ignore the way her nipples rubbed against her bra with each breath she took. Her legs trembled and her thighs ached, and none of it had to do with the ride they'd just taken. No, she couldn't help but anticipate the ride ahead.

Dillon over her, between her legs, his hands trailing over her body—

"Are you okay?" His deep voice shattered the image, pulling her back to the present, to the man standing in front of her and the distinct possibility that he didn't find her half as exciting as she found him.

Duh. You already know that. Last night was proof. Just give it up and focus on learning as much as possible. This isn't about Dillon. It's about wowing Colt Grainger, and every other available man in town.

It *was*, she told herself, ignoring a ripple of disappointment.

"Meg?" Dillon's voice pushed into her thoughts.

"Fine," she finally managed. "I'm great."

"Good. Come on." He led her several feet, the deep, husky timber of his voice guiding and coaxing, until they finally stopped and he let go of her.

"Any ideas?" he asked after several long moments.

"None that are G-rated." The words were out before she could think better of them.

A warm chuckle sizzled along her nerve endings and she felt the powerful presence in front of her. "X-rated thoughts mean you're in tune with your body, which is definitely good." The presence shifted, and suddenly she felt him next to her. "Listen to your surroundings." He continued to circle, his voice suddenly behind her. "Drink in the different scents." She heard him on her left this time. *"Feel."* He'd made a complete circle to stand in front of her again. "And tell me where you're at."

"I guess this means we're doing three lessons all at once. Which is good," she rushed on, dodging another niggle of disappointment. "Tilly announces her new list in a little over a week, which doesn't give me much time. So the quicker we get this over with, the better." *Really.* She drew a deep breath and braced herself.

She ignored the urge to reach out and set her mind to the task at hand. Her ears prickled and her nostrils flared and she concentrated on tuning in to her surroundings rather than the man who stood so close.

Too close.

The seconds ticked by. "Let's talk sounds," he finally said. "What do you hear?"

"Nothing, really." Just the steady thud of his boots on the soft earth as he circled her, the brush of denim against denim with each step, the soft in and out of his breaths.

"What about smell? You have to smell something."

"I can't actually distinguish anything." Except the detergent from his freshly laundered T-shirt, the faint whiff of aftershave. The sharp scent of desire carried on the breeze, circling her, surrounding her, along with the man himself.

"What do you feel?"

You.

The truth vibrated through her, pushing and pulling at her already tentative control. The sensations assaulted her again—the deep timbre of his voice, the raw, stirring scent of his body, the awareness that he stood right next to her, in front of her, surrounding her.

Her fingers itched and her nipples ached and she wanted to reach out more than she wanted her next breath.

"Come on, sugar," Dillon pressed. "Tell me."

"I..." She licked her lips. "I—I don't have a clue." She shook her head. "This just isn't working." She reached for the blindfold, but he stepped up behind her and caught her hands before she could pull the material from her eyes.

"Easy." The word rumbled in her ears as he checked the blindfold, his fingertips lingering at her temples, feathering over her cheeks, down the smooth column of her throat. "You're too wound up." The pad of one finger lingered at her pulse beat. "You need to relax." He drew a lazy circle against the area. "Think about something else."

His touch, so soft and rousing, played over her neck, her collarbone, and she felt some of her tension slip away. He seemed to feel it, too, and he kept going, trailing his fingertips over her shoulders. He massaged and stroked, working his way down her arms.

She barely kept from groaning. "You've got really good hands."

"You haven't seen anything yet." He kneaded her palms for several long moments before his touch drifted back up, softer this time, mesmerizing as he teased the insides of her wrists, her elbows, her biceps. Finally, his hands circled her waist. "Tell me about your first sexual encounter."

She became acutely aware of the fingers that splayed against her rib cage. A burst of panic went through her, a bubble that quickly popped and fizzled, the steady touch lulling her as much as the hypnotic stroking a moment ago. "Do I have to?"

A warm chuckle vibrated the air around them. "That bad, huh?"

"Aren't all first times?"

He stiffened. "Our first kiss *was* pretty awful."

"Awful doesn't even begin to describe it. Try rotten. Horrible. Disastrous."

"Don't be shy, sugar. Tell me what you really think." He said the words jokingly, but they were laced with a hurt that reached out and tugged at something inside of her.

"The second kiss was much better," she heard herself say. "You've definitely mastered the art."

"So have you. You have great lips. Soft. Full." *Kissable*.

The last comment slid into her ears and whispered through her head. Warmth crept through her and she felt herself relax even more.

"So," he went on. "On a scale of one to ten—" he sounded only mildly interested, but she could feel the expectancy that gripped his body "—how would you rate last night?"

"I don't know...maybe a seven."

"*Seven?*" He stiffened. "It was at least an eight."

"If it hadn't been so quick. But the short duration kicked it down a notch. If you want eight, you'll have to take your time."

"I just might do that."

The implication of his words stirred a flood of anticipation. Her tummy tingled and her heart gave a traitorous double thump.

"Forget your first time," he went on, his lips grazing her ear. "Tell me about your most memorable sexual encounter."

No. That's what she should have said. Followed by a "*Please, let's keep this arrangement as impersonal as possible. That way I won't jump you, I won't be tempted to jump you, and I won't morph into Manhandler Meg.*"

Maybe it was the blindfold that made the moment seem almost surreal and, therefore, not as threatening. Or maybe she'd proved to herself last night that she could stand strong and resist making the first move. Maybe a little of both. Either way, she heard herself murmur, "Okay."

Besides, Dillon was her friend. He always had been. He'd been there before her father had died, standing on the sidelines cheering her on when she'd tried out for the soccer team and then the baseball team, and even kicker on the boys' football team. He'd been there to console her when disaster had struck and her father had been killed. He'd gone with her to the funeral home and helped her pick out the casket and held her hand while she'd cried until she couldn't cry anymore. And he'd been there every day since, listening when she wanted to talk, reassuring her whenever she got discouraged at work.

She could tell him anything. Everything. And suddenly she wanted to.

"Set the scene. Where were you?" His deep voice filled her ears and she became instantly aware of the strong, warm hands that slid up to cup her breasts.

She had the fleeting thought that this went far beyond the usual conversation between even the best of friends, but she couldn't stop the answer that bubbled on her lips. "In my boutique."

"What did you smell?"

She took a deep breath. The sweet, intoxicating fragrance of cherries spiraled through her head, along with a dozen other distinct scents. Her nostrils flared and her chest heaved. "Fruit and chocolate and something else...a wildness, like the air when the sky's about to open up just before a big storm."

Like now.

It was *him*—his raw sexuality and insatiable hunger—that drifted through her head and teased her senses.

"What did you feel?"

"The hard counter at my back," she murmured. "Strong, purposeful hands trailing over my body." She trembled as heat swept through her.

"What else?" he prompted.

"A wetness between my legs..." Her breath caught and her legs threatened to buckle as she relived the memory for the next few moments. His lips and tongue caressing and devouring and—

"Here?" The word drew her away from the memory, back to the present and the fingertip that brushed across her crotch. A sharp bolt of desire shot from her head to the tips of her toes. She caught a gasp and bit down on her bottom lip.

"I'll take that as a *yes*."

She nodded as he circled the sensitive area with his fingertips. "Remembering a sexy encounter gets your juices flowing. It stirs you up and makes your body yearn for more." His touch drifted a delicious inch lower and his fingertips caught her hem. And then she felt him through the thin satin of her thong. He circled her before his touch drifted an inch lower and he stroked the slit between her legs. "Do you want more, Meg?"

She fought for her voice, but the soft, whispering strokes made it difficult. "I…"

"I didn't hear you, sugar." His finger went back and forth and her knees trembled. "Come on. *Tell me.*"

Her mouth opened and the frantic *yes* rushed to her lips at the same time that her brain issued a firm *don't do it!*

"You know you want me."

She did, and if she said it out loud, so would he.

She wouldn't be able to stop herself then. She would act on her want without ever knowing if the feeling was mutual. Without ever knowing if he wasn't just going along with the situation because he was horny and she was handy.

Without ever really knowing that he wanted *her*.

"I want to make the next *Hot Chicks* list," the words rushed out.

She snatched off the blindfold and found herself staring out over a blaze of twinkling lights, her toes flush with a sharp ledge high above the small town.

"Crazy Cooter's Ridge," she gasped as realization struck.

She was standing at the drop-off point where, ages ago, Cooter McWilliams had taken a nosedive to his death after his prize-winning hog, Gracie, had run away from home—hence the *crazy* tagged on to his name. Gracie had turned up a few days later, but Cooter had already taken the plunge and so the pig had inherited a shitload of money and had lived the high life at a local pet resort for several years before dying of old age. The huge cliff that overlooked the town had since become a ripe make-out spot for the local kids on the weekends.

Tonight was a school night, and so the area was deserted.

The wind licked at the tips of her bare toes peeking from her high-heeled sandals. Panic rushed through her as her mind rifled back through the past few moments. The wind whispering around her, the hands teasing her, Dillon circling her, his voice coming from one side then the other. The back and then the front—

Impossible!

She'd been in this exact spot *before* he'd started talking. Standing at the edge. There'd been no ground in front of her. No place for him to stand. To walk. To tease. Unless…

She remembered dreaming of him standing on her balcony. The way his eyes had blazed first one color and then the other. The way he seemed to always know what she was thinking, as if he could see into her thoughts and read her mind.

Yeah, sure.

Denial rushed through her. She was making something out of nothing. Maybe she was hard of hearing. Or maybe the wind had thrown her off. Or the high altitude. Or maybe she was just plain nuts.

The last one would certainly explain why no man wanted to jump her bones. Men thought women were complicated enough. Throw insane into the mix and, well, it didn't make for the most attractive package.

"I guess I get a great big zero for this lesson, don't I?" She started to turn, but he stopped her, his arms on either side of her, anchoring her in front of him.

"Not if you learned something from it."

"Such as?"

"Trust your instincts. That's the real key to being irresistible. A woman who trusts herself, who listens to her body and lets it guide her, is the ultimate in sexy. If you're feeling sexy, you act it."

"And if I don't feel sexy?" she managed to ask, despite every nerve in her body which screamed otherwise.

She needed to put some distance between them. He was too close, his chest cushioning her back, his hands anchored around her waist, fingertips burning through the thin material of her shirt. And damned if she didn't want him even closer, his hands under her shirt, between her legs.

"Don't be afraid," he said as if reading her thoughts.

"Easy for you to say," she said, her voice shaking. "If we plunge to our death, I'm going over the edge first. At least you'll have a cushion to land on. I'll be flat on the ground."

"You underneath me," he mused. "I could think of worse ways to go."

"Seriously." Her heart pounded in her chest. "I know the view is great and everything, but I really don't like this." She didn't want to like it.

To like him.

He tightened his arms around her waist. "I won't let you fall."

No, he wouldn't *let* her fall. He would push her right over the edge, and suddenly that scared her more than anything else—the notion of falling, helplessly, hopelessly, for Dillon Cash.

"I—I'm afraid of heights," she blurted. *Liar.*

He didn't move for several moments. He just stood there, his hands touching her, his body surrounding her, as if he didn't buy her explanation. As if the more he touched her, the more he could shake her control. He knew it. And so did she.

"Please," she added. *Please.*

Just like that, he let go. By the time she turned, he was already several yards away.

A strange sensation swept up her spine, but then he turned and his gaze collided with hers. Moonlight spilled down around them, outlining his powerful frame, making him seem taller, more imposing. His eyes seemed to glitter with an intensity that sucked the air from her lungs and made her heart beat even faster. "Let's go."

A trick of the light, she told herself as she forced her wobbly legs to move. She climbed on behind him, careful to keep her back straight and her hold loose as she slid her arms around his waist.

With her eyes wide-open this time, the ride back to town was even more stirring than the ride to Cooter's Ridge. Not only could she hear and smell and feel, but she could see him, as well—the wide expanse of his back, his broad shoulders, his muscular, tattooed arms. His powerful hands gripped the handlebars, his fingers flexing as he guided the bike with the controlled ease of someone who'd been riding his entire life.

He hadn't, she reminded herself. Months ago, he'd been as awkward, as uncertain, as *un*sexy as she was.

And just as desperate for a change.

She clung to the thought and tried to ignore the desire bubbling through her. A useless effort with most of her senses in major overload. One sweet, succulent taste of him and she would surely go over the edge.

The realization stuck in her head and urged her to lean forward, to trail the tip of her tongue down the side of his neck and relish the salty-sweetness of his skin...

She eased forward just an inch, her lips so close to his tempting skin.

Close, but not quite there.

Not yet.

Not ever.

Temptation pushed and pulled inside of her, threatening her fragile control. By the time he pulled up in front of her boutique, it was all she could do to pull away from him, climb off the bike and walk to the door. She could feel his gaze burning into her, but she didn't look back, not even to ask about another lesson.

Especially not to ask about another lesson.

She'd barely survived tonight with her dignity intact. The last thing she wanted to think about was facing the temptation all over again. No, she would have to come up with a different plan. The carnal classes would eventually pay off and she would have men crawling all over her. *And* she would make Tilly's list. She would just have to be patient until then and make due with her Twinkies and her fantasies.

"Tomorrow night," she heard his voice behind her as she slid her key into the lock. "I'll pick you up here."

She shook her head. "I don't think—" she started to respond, but then the engine growled, drowning out the rest of her refusal. She turned in time to see him take off down the street.

A few minutes later, Meg climbed into her own car, headed home and tried to come up with several convincing reasons to cancel.

No way was she meeting Dillon Cash tomorrow night.

She would play sick, she decided as she pulled into her driveway, climbed out of her car and headed inside the house. Maybe a rash. A fever. Maybe even some heavy-duty vomiting. Something really icky and contagious. Something that would have her lying on the floor, limp and lifeless—

Her thoughts skidded to a halt, along with her feet when she reached the kitchen doorway and spied the pile of fur that lay on the floor amid the remains of the three boxes of snack cakes Meg had picked up at the store earlier that day.

Babe was on her side, pieces of cardboard and cellophane littering the floor near her head. Crumbs clung to her whiskers, along with the scent of sugar and vanilla.

"Don't tell me you ate them all?"

The animal lifted her head and whimpered.

She'd eaten them all.

"Glutton." Meg dropped to her knees and stroked the animal's head. "I know it hurts, but I promise you'll live." But a few more whimpers and she wasn't so sure. She knew Twinkies couldn't hurt the dog.

One Twinkie.

Maybe even two.

But three dozen? Along with shreds of the plastic wrappers?

"It's okay," she murmured, gathering the large dog close.

The memories stirred and she found herself back home in the cabin where she'd grown up. She sat in the middle of the kitchen floor, a small puppy in her arms, the police officer who'd delivered the news of her father's accident standing awkwardly by as he waited for her grandparents to arrive.

Meg shook away the images and fought the sudden fear that gripped her.

A few minutes later, she loaded Babe into the backseat of her car, climbed behind the wheel and headed for the nearest twenty-four-hour animal clinic.

12

SHIT. SHIT. *SHIT*.

Dillon skidded to a stop in the parking lot of Skull Creek Choppers and killed the engine. Climbing off the bike, he stomped to the back door, his body stiff and tight. His gut clenched and unclenched as he shoved the key into the lock and threw open the door.

Inside, he bypassed the office and strode into the manufacturing shop. It was still early in the evening—barely 10:00 p.m.—and so the place was empty. Garret was out with whatever woman he'd taken a fancy to and Jake was with Nikki. Both vampires were no doubt drinking their fill in more ways than one.

A pang of hunger gripped him. His hands trembled, his muscles flexed and his jaw clenched. As worked up as he was, he wasn't about to try to park himself behind a desk and worry about his blog or his leads or even the Ancient One himself.

He needed to *do* something.

Hitting the power button, he fired up the high-tech computer terminal that he'd set up near the main tool table. The screen flickered to life and a 3-D image of a custom-made chopper appeared.

Dillon had entered the specifics for Garret's next order and the end result was the beauty on the monitor. His gaze shifted to the worktable and the simple frame that would eventually transform into the chopper.

Punching up several measurements, he surveyed the spreadsheet that scrolled across the screen. Following the details, he powered on the ARC welder and turned his attention to the hulk of metal that would soon be the custom-made fuel tank.

He spent the next few minutes working on the piece and trying not to think about Meg.

She was scared, all right. But it wasn't of heights.

She was scared of falling in love, of being in love.

With him.

And the problem is?

He had her right where he wanted her. If he tempted and teased her just a little more, he had no doubt she would make the first move. And the second. And the third.

She would offer herself up to him completely and he would get what he wanted—the chance to break Bobby's record and be remembered, not as the ultimate geek, but as the most legendary lover in town.

If.

Wait a second, there was no *if*. It was all about *when*.

Tomorrow night.

As for her fear of falling in love with him… He simply had to be reading her wrong. When she looked at him, she felt lust. Because of her past, she was afraid to act on that lust, afraid to perpetuate her own reputation.

Lust.

That's all she felt for him and all he felt for her. So he'd obviously been hallucinating. Since turning, he hadn't gone a full twenty-four hours without sex. He was going on seventy-two and lack of sustenance was making him punchy.

He needed to feed.

Tonight.

Now.

The thought struck as he saw a flash of lights through the window. He glanced up in time to see Meg's car haul ass past the shop.

Urgency spiraled through him, a feeling that had nothing to do with his own damned hunger and everything to do with the woman he'd just glimpsed. Her tear-streaked face. Her fear-filled eyes.

Something was wrong.

So? It doesn't matter. All you feel is lust, remember?

But it wasn't. They were friends, too.

Friends first.

And so Dillon did what any friend would do. He climbed on his motorcycle and hauled ass after her.

MEG FORCED HERSELF TO let go and handed Babe over to the night staff at Junction Animal Hospital. Her heart pounded painfully in her chest and her throat tightened as she watched her dog disappear through the double doors leading to the emergency exam room.

"You can have a seat." The woman behind the desk motioned Meg over to a small cluster of chairs, most of the seats already overflowing with worried pet owners. "It's a full moon, so we've had a busy night. Mr. McKinley's Jack Russell's got into a fight with a porcupine. Stu Morehead's rabbit, Fluffy, got her paw caught in some chicken wire. Jimmy Carmichael's prize-winning Arabian broke his leg near a gulley out by Old Sam's Creek and Agnes Carmichael's Great Dane ate one of her slippers." The woman smiled. "Just relax and help yourself to some complimentary coffee. This might take awhile."

Meg walked over to an empty chair, but a full thirty seconds later she was on her feet again. She paced a small area off to the side, in front of the coffee machine, and tried to fight the worry mounting inside of her. The scent of disinfectant filled her nostrils and dread settled in the pit of her stomach.

She had to be okay.

"She will be." Dillon's deep voice slid into Meg's ears a split second before she felt his strong, warm hand on her shoulder.

His presence seemed to wrap around her. The scent of warm male tinged her nostrils and an inexplicable wildness filled her head, chasing away the sharp odor of Lysol and animal fur that hung heavy in the air. She glanced up and her gaze met his. His green eyes gleamed with a certainty that eased her frantic heart beat. A strange sense of peace stole through her, pushing aside her worry and fear.

"She'll be okay," he said again as if he knew she needed his reassurance more than she needed her next breath.

And for the first time since leaving the house, Meg started to think that he just might be right.

"BASICALLY, SHE JUST ATE too much," Doc Jamison told Meg an hour later.

They stood in the doorway of one of the exam rooms. Inside, Babe lay on a large steel table. Dillon stood next to the animal and stroked her soft fur. Babe's leg gave an excited shake and relief swamped Meg.

"She has a bad case of indigestion," the vet went on. "A very bad case what with all the plastic she ingested on top of the sugar."

"But she's going to be okay, right? You'll give her some Tums and send her home."

"More than settling her stomach, we want to get her to pass everything, so she has a busy night ahead. You'll have to watch her, too, and keep her out of the pantry tonight. Otherwise, I might have to pump her stomach. That's as painful for dogs as it is for humans."

Meg nodded. "No more Twinkies."

"Or anything that isn't on this list." He handed over a neatly typed list of appropriate foods, along with at-home care instructions. "Don't give her anything tonight, but once she passes everything, she'll need nourishment. Namely, plenty of protein. I'm also going to give her a little something to ease the cramps. If you follow Shirley, there—" the vet motioned to the woman next to him who'd been sitting at the front desk "—she'll get you all taken care of."

Meg left Babe with Dillon and followed Shirley back through the double doors and out to the front desk. Five minutes later, she had a full bottle of pain pills along with a bottle of powdered fiber that she was supposed to mix and feed to Babe once they got home.

Meg took a deep breath as the news sank in. *Indigestion.* Not a heart attack or a stroke or any of the other horrible things she'd imagined might result from sponge cake overload.

"She's going to be okay."

Dillon's deep, reassuring words echoed in her head a split second before he appeared next to her, Babe cradled in his arms.

"I think she's starting to feel better," he murmured, nuzzling the dog.

Babe rewarded him with a lick on the cheek and Meg realized that Babe was just as susceptible to him as every other female in Skull Creek.

Every female, that is, except Meg herself.

The knowledge should have been comforting—she was standing strong, holding her own, waiting to be ravished rather than making a fool of herself and acting on her own one-sided lust. Instead, she couldn't help but feel as if she was missing out on the chance of a lifetime.

His deep voice pushed into her thoughts. "Ready?"

In more ways than one, she realized as she followed him out to her car and watched him load Babe into the backseat. He gave the animal another affectionate scrub behind her ears and Babe's tail twitched. She liked Dillon, and so did Meg. And she was *ready,* all right, to head home, to give in, to let go.

The notion stuck in her head and warred with her determination as she made the drive back to her place, Dillon following on his motorcycle. Once they pulled up in her driveway, he gathered Babe from the car and toted her inside.

A few minutes later, Meg watched him lay the animal on a batch of fluffy quilts that she'd pulled from the closet, and suddenly she wasn't half as scared to make the first move with him as she was *not* to make the first move.

To feel his arms around her and his lips eating at hers and his body so deep she didn't know where he ended and she began.

To lose herself in the sweet heat she'd been fighting since

she'd come face-to-face with the new and improved Dillon Cash just a few days ago.

And backslide into Manhandler Meg?

The question struck, reminding her of the past and her own reputation, and the all-important fact that she was still desperate to erase both.

Throwing herself at Dillon Cash would accomplish nothing.

At the same time, it was the one thing she wanted most at the moment. The only thing.

She busied herself for the next few minutes giving Babe her medication and getting her settled for the night. With each movement, she felt Dillon's gaze and while the tension between them was thick, there was something oddly comforting about having him there. She didn't feel so alone.

He'd been her friend back when she'd needed one most. And he'd been her friend tonight when she'd needed one most.

All the more reason to resist the crazy thoughts racing through her head.

"I should be going," he said.

Let him, her conscience urged. *Otherwise you'll regret it tomorrow.*

"Thanks for showing up at the animal hospital." She started for the front door.

"That's what friends are for." He followed behind her, so close she could feel the warmth of his body, the tightness of his muscles, the rush of his breath ruffling the hair on her head. Her skin prickled and her nipples throbbed and she felt the moisture between her legs. Her memory stirred and his voice echoed, so clear and distinct, it seemed he whispered them at that particular moment.

A woman who trusts herself, who listens to her body and lets it guide her, is the ultimate in sexy.

She turned on him. Their gazes collided. Surprise registered on his face as her hands went to the bottom of her blouse. Before she could breathe, let alone give in to the insecurity whirling inside of her, she whisked the material up and over her head.

By the time her gaze met his again, his eyes had fired to a fierce, glittering green. She felt a niggle of apprehension because as right as everything was, it wasn't. There was something different about him. Something that went beyond his sexy appearance and newfound confidence. Something dark and dangerous.

The notion struck as he stared at her, into her, but then his gaze dropped to her breasts and she forgot everything except the desire swamping her.

Lifting her hands, she worked at the bra clasp until it snapped and popped. The cups fell away and the scrap of lingerie landed at her feet. Her skirt soon slouched in a heap around her ankles and she stood before him wearing nothing but a pink thong. She hooked her thumbs at the waistband, slid the satin down her legs and stepped free. Just like that she was completely naked.

She felt a moment's hesitation as she stood there, but then he murmured, "You're so damned beautiful," and it was all the encouragement she needed.

Closing the distance between them, she reached for the hem of his T-shirt. He lifted his arms, letting her pull the cotton up and over his head. Where she'd seen him bare-chested back at the motel a few days ago, the sight of him now was a hundred times better.

Muscles carved his torso, from his bulging biceps and shoulders to the rippled plane of his abdomen. Gold, silky hair sprinkled his chest, narrowing to a tiny whorl of silk that disappeared beneath the waistband of his jeans.

She meant to slow down, to at least let him do something, but she couldn't help herself. She reached out and pressed her palm against his chest, feeling the hair tickle her skin. She followed the golden path lower until it stopped at his waistband.

He balled his hands into fists at his sides, as if it took everything he had not to cover her hand with his and urge her lower, wanting her to take the lead.

And where she would have stood her ground and tried to hold back a few moments ago, she'd already waved the white flag and given up.

She'd lost the battle with her own damned lust.

Oddly enough, she felt more like a winner than a loser as she dropped to her knees in front of him and reached for the waistband of his pants. The zipper hissed and he sprang hot and eager into her hands. She trailed her fingers over him, tracing the bulging veins until she reached the ripe, plump head of his penis. He stiffened and a drop of pearly liquid beaded at the tip. She leaned forward, closed her lips around the smooth ridge and lapped at his essence with her tongue for a long sweet moment before she felt his hands on her shoulders.

"Don't."

Her gaze met his and where she expected him to look victorious, instead he looked more startled.

"What's wrong?"

"Nothing." The word was raw and thick. He shook his head and the strange look faded into one of hungry determination. He pulled her to her feet and his mouth claimed hers in a deep, thorough kiss that took her breath away.

Dillon plunged his tongue deep, tangling with hers as he tried to understand what the hell had just happened to him.

Or rather, what had *almost* happened.

One draw of her sweet mouth on his cock and he'd been ready to explode. *Just like that.* Like some wet-behind-the-ears virgin. Like the town geek experiencing his first blow job.

The thing was, it wasn't his first and he certainly wasn't a virgin. And he sure as hell wasn't a geek, no matter how much a tiny voice inside of him screamed otherwise.

He was a vampire who thrived on sex.

He didn't get off until the woman got off. It was her climax—the sweet, dizzying energy—that seeped into him, stirred his hunger and sent him over the edge.

Not this time.

Not with Meg.

Because she's the ultimate challenge.

The explanation whispered through his head, easing the

anxiety that rushed through him. This was his moment of truth, and so it made sense that he would be a little out of sorts. On top of that, he was hungry.

So damned hungry.

He fought against the urge to push her up against the nearest wall and bury himself inside of her. Instead, he eased the pressure of his mouth and shifted the kiss from fast and furious to slow and wicked and thorough.

His tongue tangled with hers and he ate at her mouth. She stiffened at first, as if unsure as to the sudden change, but then she relaxed, sucking on his tongue, giving as good as she got.

It was the most passionate kiss of her life.

The most stirring.

The most unnerving.

He felt it as his hands slid down her trembling body, tracing the curve of her spine, kneading her sweet ass for several long moments until she clutched at his shoulders and slumped against him.

Sweeping her into his arms, he headed upstairs, down the hall, into her bedroom. Moonlight pushed through the French doors, filling the room with an ethereal light that bathed her flawless skin as he stretched her out on her cotton candy-pink sheets.

He didn't bother taking his jeans off or sinking to the bed beside her. As determined as he was, he didn't trust himself. His gut clenched too tightly, the hunger too fierce. The sharpness of his fangs grazed his tongue and electricity sizzled through him.

Easy.

"Dillon?" Her soft voice drew his attention.

She stared up at him, her lips full and slick from his mouth, her nipples ripe, her breasts flushed, her legs open. Her cleft was wet and swollen and desire knifed through him, along with a pang of hunger so fierce it stalled his heart for several fast, furious seconds.

"I want you," she murmured, as if she thought he waited just to hear the words.

That was exactly what she thought, he realized as he stared

deep into her eyes and saw the rush of uncertainty, the flash of defeat. His chest tightened and something shifted inside of him. Suddenly it wasn't about his own damned hunger, but hers.

"No." He leaned over her and slid a finger into her pulsing heat. "I want you." And then he captured her mouth with his.

Over the next few minutes, he stroked and tasted and drove her to the brink of orgasm. He plunged his tongue deep, mimicking the action with his fingers, in and out, deeper and deeper, until she whimpered and tugged at his jeans.

But he was a man on a mission and so he caught her hands and pushed them up over her head. He placed a long, lingering kiss on her lips before trailing his mouth over her jaw and down the side of her neck. Her pulse beat against his lips and his groin tightened. Heat swept through him and he trembled. He felt the sharp edge of his teeth graze her fragrant flesh. Once. Twice.

She gasped, the sound like a loud *pop* in his head that yanked him back to reality. He licked the tiny scrape he'd made on her skin and moved on, kissing and nibbling until he reached her breasts. He lapped at her ripe nipple before blowing on the tip and making her moan.

Her fingers threaded through his hair and held him to her as he drew her deep and sucked her long and hard. He heard her pulse beat in his head, throbbing against his mouth, and it took everything he had not to sink his fangs deep and feel the warmth flowing into his mouth at the same time he felt her tight, hot body close around his cock.

His mouth closed over hers again as he trailed a hand down, over her breast, her abdomen, until he reached her slick folds. He touched her again and she gasped. A drop of warmth spurted over his knuckle and trailed across his palm. His gut tightened and he grew harder, hotter, hungrier.

He slid a finger deep, relishing the incredible heat that sucked at him. With each thrust, the pressure built, pushing her higher until her eyes glazed over and her cheeks flushed. Another deep, dizzying thrust and suddenly she was there.

Her nails dug into his shoulders and she arched off the bed. A moan burst from her lips and he caught it, absorbing the sound the way he absorbed the delicious energy that rushed through him, quieting the roaring in his ears.

But there was none of the usual satisfaction that he usually felt at this point.

Just the fierce need for more.

For her.

He stood and kicked off his boots. Shoving his jeans and underwear down, he kicked them aside then joined her on the bed. He pushed her legs even wider, pulling them up at the knees to give himself better access. The head of his penis pushed a delicious inch into her sweet heat and pleasure spiked through him—

"Wait!" Her soft plea pushed past the sudden roaring in his ears and his gaze collided with hers. "A condom," she gasped. "We need a condom."

He hadn't had much need for protection during the past few months. Vampires couldn't catch anything—not with the mother of all viruses already flowing through their veins. Nor could they give anything. Passing on his vampness involved sharing his blood, not his body. As for making little vamp babies, that was pretty much impossible according to Garret.

But Meg didn't know any of that, and Dillon had no intention of letting her know he wasn't really half as sexy as she thought. It was his vamp charisma.

Here today, gone tomorrow.

A pang of regret washed through him, followed by a rush of *so?* Who cared why she wanted him so badly. The fact was, she did want him.

Badly.

He focused on the thought and reached for his jeans and the ancient condom that had been in his wallet since junior high. Tearing at the foil packet, he rolled the latex on in one swift motion, he pressed her down into the mattress and settled between her legs. The head of his erection slid along her damp flesh and she shuddered. Her soft, wet folds sucked at the very tip of his head and he groaned.

"Wrap your legs around me," he finally managed to whisper, his voice husky and raw.

Her legs snaked around his waist. The motion lifted her and he slid deep. Usually he paused at this point, relishing the heat, building the anticipation because he drew the most energy when a woman came apart in his arms.

But then he felt the same rush of desperation he'd felt when she'd taken him into her mouth, and he couldn't control himself.

He started to move, penetrating deeply with each plunge of his cock. His hands played over her body, feeling every curve and indentation. The feel of her roused him as much as the sight of her spread beneath him, her head flung back, her eyes closed, her lips parted, her body lifting to meet the thrust of his hips.

Catching the tip of one nipple between his lips, he sucked her in, drawing on her, feeling her soft flesh graze his fangs as he moved in and out. Her muscles tightened around him and her body went tense as he slid free. Another deep thrust and she exploded. She milked him as the ecstasy gripped her. Heat rippled through him, sating his hunger and feeding his own energy. He forced his mouth from her breast and stared down at her, drinking in the picture that she made lost in the throes of orgasm.

Her face and neck were flushed, her lips parted and trembling, her eyes glittering.

His hunger roared to life and suddenly, he couldn't plunge fast enough, deep enough. He tried, pushing and withdrawing and...there. Yes, *there!*

Pleasure splintered his brain and his body convulsed. He felt his gaze brighten and blaze.

"What the—"

Her soft voice pushed past the beating in his skull and lifted the haze of pleasure long enough for him to see the shock on her face as she stared up at him, into him.

He clamped his eyes shut and gave her a plundering, consuming kiss meant to distract her from what she'd just seen.

Or what she'd thought she'd seen.

No way could it have been real.

At least that's what she told herself. Denial rushed through her, easing her panic until she forgot everything save kissing him back.

Thankfully.

Otherwise, Garret would have his ass.

At least that's what Dillon told himself as he rolled onto his back and stared up at the ceiling, his heart pounding, his blood rushing. No way did he want to consider the possibility that he didn't want her to know because he actually liked her and wanted her to like him. *Now and tomorrow.* And if she knew the truth, she would surely write off her attraction as a result of his vamp charisma.

And she'd be right.

He ignored a pang of regret and tried to focus on the sweet rush of victory that spiraled through him.

He'd broken Bobby's record.

Instead of being the town's biggest geek, he would now go down in the history books as Skull Creek's most legendary lover.

Unfortunately, the truth didn't make him feel half as good as Meg did when she snuggled into his embrace, closed her eyes and fell asleep.

A realization that pushed him to his feet and had him reaching for his pants and boots. A few minutes later, he hit the front door, climbed onto his motorcycle and got the hell out of there.

Because no way was Dillon falling in love with her.

His life—or lack of—was way too complicated as it was. The last thing he needed was to muck it up with a relationship that didn't stand a chance in hell, heaven or the in-between.

13

MEG LISTENED AS THE rumble of Dillon's motorcycle faded in the distance. She barely resisted the urge to rush to the French doors and catch one last glimpse of him.

Instead, she slid her hand to the indentation he'd made next to her. The warmth seeped into her fingers and his lingering scent teased her nostrils.

"I want you."

His admission echoed in her head, but it did little to curb the disappointment creeping through her.

Because she'd given in first.

That's what she told herself. No way would she even consider the alternative—that she missed Dillon. That she felt more for him than mutual respect or friendship or simple like.

Ditto for all three, but nothing more. She certainly hadn't *fallen* for him.

Not even a little.

She'd been tired and upset and horny, and the three had made for a dangerous combination. Of course, she'd gone a little nuts. The guy was hot, sexy, irresistible, and so she'd caved.

But no more. She'd had enough sex to last her another six months and she was no longer terrified that she might lose Babe. A little sleep, and she would have her wits about her.

Tomorrow morning, she would wake up and get back in the game. Back to searching for a way to beef up her sex appeal and make Tilly's coveted list.

Without Dillon Cash.

She couldn't continue their lessons even if he wanted to—and she had her doubts considering the fact that he'd left without so much as a see ya. While she hadn't fallen for him yet, she wasn't going to take any chances.

It would be too easy.

And too heartbreaking.

Despite his admission, she knew he didn't feel the same I-have-to-have-you-right-now-or-I'll-die passion that she felt for him. Otherwise, he wouldn't have been able to hold back for so long. No, he'd teased and taunted the past few days and she had no doubt that, had she not made the first move, tonight would have ended like all the others—sexless and frustrating.

Regret washed through her and she stiffened. She pushed to her feet. A delicious ache spiraled through her along with several vivid, very graphic memories of the past hour. Her hands trembled and her legs shook and heat chased up and down her skin.

Yep, tomorrow she was back on the wagon.

As for tonight...

She headed for the bathroom and an ice-cold shower.

"Looks like someone didn't get much sleep last night," Terry remarked when Meg walked into work fifteen minutes late the next morning.

It was the same comment she'd heard from Doris Milligan when she'd stopped at the coffee shop for a double cappuccino with a shot of espresso. And from old Mr. Parker when she'd stopped at the Quick Stop for a copy of the latest *In Style*.

It was as if the entire world could tell with one glance that she'd had wild and crazy sex last night with Mr. Wild & Crazy himself.

"It wasn't anything serious," she blurted, telling Terry the same thing she'd been telling herself since Dillon had walked away last night. "We're just friends."

"I wasn't talking about you. I'm talking about me again." The woman hefted an armload of dresses to a nearby rack. "I swear I didn't get so much as a solid ten minutes." She reached

for the protein drink sitting on a nearby table and took a long
swig. "And I'm definitely feeling it this morning."

Meg set her purse on the shelf near a stack of Brighton leather
belts and headed for the cluster of boxes to help Terry unpack.
"Anyone I know?"

The woman shook her head. "Hank."

"Don't tell me you slept with him *again?*"

"I didn't sleep with him." She shook her head. "But he wants
me to. He called all night long, first while I was trying to work
out on my elliptical trainer. Then while I was on the treadmill.
Then during my favorite *Move Those Buns* DVD. Then while I
was scarfing down a double cheese and sausage pizza."

"You don't scarf pizza. You don't scarf anything."

"I do after eighteen phone calls from Hank."

"Eighteen?" Meg noted the worried glimmer in Terry's brown
eyes and suddenly her own troubles didn't seem all that terrible.
"Maybe you should call Sheriff Matthews."

"And tell him what? That I slept with my ex and now he
wants a repeat?" She shook her head. "Hank's just lonely, that's
all. Since we broke up, he hasn't had a relationship that's lasted
over two months."

"Because he's a jerk."

"True."

"A jerk who's harassing you." Meg reached for a box cutter.
"You should call the sheriff."

"He just wants to talk. He hasn't threatened or yelled, or
done anything."

Yet.

The silent word hung between them for several long moments
before Terry finally shook her head.

"I know Hank. He'll give it up eventually. He always does."
She summoned a smile. "I swear the man couldn't stay focused
long enough to hold a job or give me a decent orgasm. He'll move
on to something else." She waved a hand. "In the meantime, I
just have to hold tight and keep from encouraging him."

Kimberly Raye 145

"And try not to gain thirty pounds in the process."

"You aren't kidding." She pinched at her waist before turning her attention to the boxes. She sliced open one box while Meg tackled another. A few seconds later, she unearthed a black sports jacket and let loose a low whistle. "Since when do we carry anything like this?"

"I've had a few requests for men's clothes, so I thought I'd have a some samples on hand just in case anyone is interested." Meg shrugged and ignored the sudden ache between her legs. "It's all in the name of good business."

"And here I thought it was all in the name of Dillon Cash."

Meg's head snapped up. "What are you talking about?"

"Come on, Meg. The entire town knows that you and Dillon are seeing each other. Margie Culpepper's daughter Dana saw you two out riding around last night. And Camille Harlingen's grandmother was out walking her dog and saw you two here at the boutique the night before that." Terry gave her a knowing look. "Either you guys are seeing each other, or Grandma Harlingen's doing more with that cooking sherry than making pot roast."

Meg's mind rifled back through the past hour. She'd had a ton of knowing looks while she'd been in line for her coffee. And even more at the Quick Stop.

Because they know.

Her hands trembled as she searched for her most nonchalant voice. "What, um, exactly did she see?"

"Enough to have you halfway down the aisle because you're carrying his baby."

"You're kidding, right?"

Terry shrugged. "You're a woman and he's a man. You were in the same room together and, if Grandma Harlingen's bifocals are still the right prescription, you were minus your undies."

"That still doesn't mean we had sex." *Not here.*

"Maybe not, though I can't for the life of me imagine that you would go undie-less and not jump Dillon Cash." She waved a hand. "But even if you didn't, Mabel's told everyone you're the reincarnation of Jezebel, so you might as well have."

"Who exactly did she tell?"

"Her Bunko group at the senior center. And you know that's as good as telling every person in this town." Terry grinned. "Looks like I might have some competition for next week's list."

Hope fired inside of Meg, dispelling her sudden embarrassment. "You really think so?"

"One more date with Dillon and I'm old news."

Terry's words were like a rush of wind and just like that, the hope died. "I wouldn't write a goodbye speech just yet." At the woman's questioning look, Meg added, "I'm not seeing him again."

Terry arched an eyebrow. "That bad, huh?"

That good.

Meg could still remember the feel of his skin beneath hers, his hands roaming her body, his hips pumping furiously, his penis plunging deep. Her cheeks heated. "I wouldn't exactly say he was *bad*. It just wasn't what I expected." It was more, which meant she couldn't—wouldn't—go out with Dillon again, not even for the sake of Tilly's list.

She tamped down a rush of disappointment and tried to focus on the positive. The lessons, however few, had obviously worked. She'd finally reached Jezebel status.

The trick now was to figure out a way to keep it, at least for the next week until Tilly announced her new list.

Her mind raced and rifled through dozens of possibilities as she turned her attention to unpacking merchandise. She'd just pulled a pair of Gucci silver slingbacks from a mound of tissue paper when genius seemed to strike.

If being seen with the town's hottest guy had upped her sex factor that much, then being seen with another guy—not as *yowza* as Dillon when it came to sex appeal, but still a respectable *wow*—might solidify it.

The notion struck and she almost pushed it back out. The

sudden thought of being with a good-looking man, touching him, kissing him, didn't stir the same excitement that it usually did.

Because of Dillon.

He wasn't just a hot guy. He was a double whammy—a hot guy and her friend, and last night she'd realized just how dangerous to her control such a combination could be.

Still, she'd come too far to give up now.

She reached for the phone and dialed the local real estate office. "Colt Grainger, please," she said when the receptionist picked up.

"This is Meg," she said when she heard his deep *"Yes?"* "I'd rather not wait until next Saturday. Why don't we see each other tonight?"

FOR THE FIRST TIME IN two months, Dillon Cash was alone on a Friday night.

He sat at the bar, a bottle of beer in front of him, a lively two-step number bouncing off the walls around him. The Roundup was one of about a half-dozen honky tonks that lined the interstate between Skull Creek and Junction.

The perfect place to pick up a warm, willing woman.

All he had to do was scope out the sea of hot bodies that filled the dance floor and pick whichever one caught his fancy. A blond bombshell with a nice ass or a brunette with big breasts or a redhead with long legs.

The trouble was, he'd already slept with most everyone in the place, and so he'd settled for a beer.

He took a deep swig of Coors, but the liquid didn't ease the tightening in his gut or sate the thirst that clawed at his throat. He needed to feed, to drink in enough sweet, rich blood to fortify him on top of the heavy dose of sex he'd had last night.

Then he could think again.

Concentrate.

He had a ton of things on his plate right now—the handlebars he'd started last night on the new chopper, his blog, the background checks on his list of possible Joes. Which meant he should give it up, head for a spot farther down the interstate where there were sure to be a few new faces, and get busy.

He knew it, but damned if he could make himself move. Instead, he downed another swig of beer and wished with all his heart that he could punch something.

His gaze fixed on the woman currently two-stepping her way across the dance floor with another man.

His woman.

She wore a brown leather vest that didn't have anything underneath it except skin, and a pair of tight, stonewashed jeans. Add a pair of high heeled cowboy boots, her jeans stuffed inside, and Meg Sweeney was definitely the hottest thing on two legs.

But her appeal went deeper than the clothes. Her long, blond hair was slightly mussed and flowed down around her shoulders. Her eyes sparkled. Her skin glowed. She looked as if she'd just rolled out of bed after a night of incredible sex.

Which wouldn't have been a problem if she'd been with the man responsible for said night.

Dillon downed another gulp and barely resisted the urge to haul ass across the room and inform her that she was making a fool of herself.

Why, she was hanging all over the guy.

Her arms looped around his neck. A smile tilted her full lips as she drank in his every word. She slid this way and that, her boots kicking up sawdust as she danced and had the time of her life.

She looked happy, vibrant, and completely oblivious to Dillon.

Not that he cared. Hell, no. Last night had been his final challenge and he'd proved himself. She'd been all over him, and she was now history.

End of story.

Bye-bye.

Sexually, that is. They were still friends. Hell, he'd sat at the vet half the friggin' night for her and he'd even dropped by her place on the way to The Roundup just to see if Babe was feeling better. Meg hadn't been home, of course, and so she hadn't known he'd sat for a full fifteen minutes, talking and petting the animal who'd toddled out her doggie door to see him until he'd felt certain the dog was on her way to a full recovery. Still. He was thoughtful and considerate and, basically, a great friend. The least she could do was look at him.

And if she doesn't know you're here?

That thought bothered him even more than the notion that she just didn't want to acknowledge him.

They'd slept together, for Christ's sake. He could still feel her hot, tight body pulsing around him. He could hear the soft breaths that sawed past her lips and the excited beat of her heart. He could smell the intoxicating aroma of warm, sweet woman. Her memory haunted him.

She, on the other hand, wasn't sparing him a second thought. Otherwise she would have looked as bad as he felt.

So much for leaving a lasting impression.

No, he was the one left with the impressions and damned if he'd had a moment's peace since he'd walked away from her. There'd been no consuming sleep that day. No smothering blackness to rejuvenate him. Instead, he'd tossed and turned and mentally kicked his own ass for leaving so abruptly.

He should have written a note or said goodbye or something.

But the *something* he'd had in mind had involved a lot more kissing and touching and so he'd gotten the hell out of there.

No seconds.

Garret had warned him and Dillon knew what would happen should he violate the rules. He'd barely made it out without biting her last night. He wouldn't be able to stop himself the next time. He would sink his fangs in as easily as he sank his cock deep, and the damage would be done.

They would be forever linked.

Like Jake and Nikki.

A pang of envy shot through him. One he quickly ignored by

downing the rest of his beer. He wasn't Jake. When the cowboy reclaimed his humanity, he would still be the ultra-cool guy he was now and Nikki would still be in love with him.

But Dillon...

He would go back to his life before and he already knew that Meg didn't find that guy the least bit attractive. As for her falling in love with him... That was an even bigger long shot than Roxy Thompson agreeing to dance with Herman Tremaine.

Dillon's gaze shifted to the short man picking his way through a maze of tables toward a tall, leggy brunette wearing a miniskirt and tube top.

Herman was six years younger and while Dillon didn't know the man personally, he knew he'd been president of the chess club and the captain of the chemistry team, and he'd gone to the state spelling bee championships both his junior and senior year, an accomplishment that no one other than Dillon, himself, could claim. Meanwhile, Roxy had been homecoming queen and dance squad commander. She'd since gone on to pose in three different Hooters calendars and had done a recent commercial for the local Piggly Wiggly. She'd also made eight out of the last ten Hot Chicks list.

Dillon's ears prickled. The music and laughter faded as he tuned into Herman's trembling voice.

"Hi, Roxy."

"Hey," she murmured. Her forehead wrinkled. *"Do I know you?"*

"I'm Herman. We went to grade school together. And junior high. And high school. We work together." When she didn't look anymore clued in, he added, *"At the bank."*

"You're a teller, too?"

"A loan officer."

"Oh."

"I, um, was thinking maybe we could, you know, dance or something. If you want," he rushed on. *"We don't have to. It's just a thought. But since the music's pretty good and you're not*

*dancing with anyone and I'm not dancing with anyone, I figure
we could dance with each other. That is, if you want."*

"Sorry, Harry. My feet are really hurting."

"It's Herman."

*"That's what I meant." She touched her temples. "And I've
got this splitting headache, too," she added before turning to her
friends and putting her back to him.*

*"Okay." He shifted nervously. "Um, well, I guess I'll see you
at work tomorrow then." He turned and her soft voice followed,
"Not if I see you first."*

Talk about a crash and burn. One that hit much too close to
home. Dillon had dealt with the same rejection for most of his
life, and he had no doubt he would deal with it again.

It was just a matter of time.

All the more reason to push last night completely out of his
head and get his ass out of here.

His gut tightened and his stomach grumbled.

He was hungry.

That was the only reason he was thinking such crazy thoughts,
like how Jake and Nikki seemed so happy and how he might—
if he tried really hard—be able to explain things to his parents
in a way that wouldn't send his mother to an early grave. And
how maybe, just maybe, he might forget all about finding the
Ancient One, and he and Meg might forge their own bond.

Too late, a voice whispered. That same voice that had played
at the back of his head all evening, reminding him of the strange
woman who'd been asking around town about him.

She'd been at it again today. Nikki had left a message on his
cell while he'd been in the shower.

"She's still here."

But even if she hadn't warned him, Dillon would have known.

He couldn't shake the awareness that rippled up and down his
spine, the certainty that someone was there. Watching. Waiting. And
while Dillon had meant to hunt down the Ancient One, he couldn't
shake the feeling that, instead, he'd somehow drawn him out.

That he'd drawn him *here*.

Uneasiness rushed down his spine and he felt a tap on his shoulder. He put on his most charming grin and gave a polite "Thanks, but not right now" to the woman who'd come up behind him. She was the cousin of a cousin of a cousin visiting for the weekend and the only woman in the entire place—with the exception of Bobby Sue Montgomery who was here with her husband, Walt, celebrating their twenty-fifth anniversary—that Dillon hadn't slept with.

She was sex trophy, pretty with pouty lips and long, dark hair and a curvy figure and he forced himself to take a second look. Other than the slow, steady rumble gnawing at his gut, he didn't feel even a ripple of desire for her.

Nothing intense.

Nothing like what he'd felt last night.

He signaled the bartender to bring him a second round before shifting his gaze back to Meg.

The minute his attention fixed on her, she stiffened and missed a step. She teetered and the man caught her. His hands slithered around her waist and he pulled her close and—

No.

Hell, no.

He pushed to his feet and, just like that, Dillon forgot the hunger raging inside of him and gave in to a fierce swell of possessiveness.

Regardless of what happened tomorrow, right now, at this moment, Meg Sweeney was his.

He knew it.

She knew it.

And it was high time everyone else knew, as well.

14

Don't look.

Meg told herself that for the countless time since Dillon Cash had walked into The Roundup and turned what should have been the most exciting night of her life—Tilly was here, cloistered at a table in the far corner with a group from the *Skull Creek Gazette* and Colt Grainger was practically drooling all over her—into an agonizing exercise in self-control.

Don't even think about looking.

She ignored the urge to turn toward the bar and the man who'd been warming the stool for the last half hour, tightened her hold on Colt's neck, stared up into his eyes and kept swaying. And smiling.

The trouble was, she didn't have to look to know that Dillon was headed straight for her. She saw him out of the corner of her eye, a black shadow that pushed up from the barstool, bisected the dance floor and closed the distance between them. Even more, she could *feel* him.

Her skin prickled and heat skittered up and down her spine. It was all she could do not to turn when she he stepped up behind her.

"We need to talk," his deep voice slid into her ears, pushing aside the music and laughter and the frantic beat of her heart.

She stiffened against the urge to turn, wrap her arms around his neck and see if he tasted half as delicious as she remembered. But she was with Colt, she reminded herself, twining her fingers around the man's neck and giving him an apologetic smile. "I'm really busy," she told Dillon.

But Dillon wasn't giving up so easily. "It'll only take a few minutes."

"I'm on a date."

"I can see that." He sounded none too pleased and a traitorous slither of hope went through her. Ridiculous because regardless of what he had to say, she knew what her answer would be—a great big no. No more lessons. No more sex.

She wasn't blowing a friendship over a few hours of mindless pleasure.

Even phenomenal mindless pleasure.

She wasn't losing Dillon, too.

"Give me five minutes."

"And miss my favorite song?" She gave Colt another *Sorry about this* smile. "I love George Strait."

"This is Tim McGraw."

"Close enough."

"Look, buddy. The lady doesn't want to talk to you," Colt cut in. "So get lost."

"Mind your own business."

"This is my…" Colt stared past her and his words faded, along with his expression. A strange light glimmered in his eyes and then they became empty. It was as if he'd spaced out. His hands loosened on her waist and fell away.

"Colt?" She stared into his blank expression. "Are you okay?"

"He's fine. Let's go."

"No." She snapped her fingers in front of Colt and waved a hand. *Nothing.* "Colt?"

"I mean it, Meg. You've got five seconds to move."

"Or what?"

"Or I'm carrying you out of here."

Before she could draw her next breath, Dillon caught her arm and whirled her around. "Time's up." He hooked her knees and folded her over his shoulder, and in the blink of an eye she found herself dangling upside down.

Meg squealed and dozens of curious stares swiveled their way.

But Dillon didn't care. He strode toward the nearest Exit. He hit the bar on the door, carried her out behind the building to the gravel lot where the employees parked and dropped her to her feet.

She blinked away a sudden rush of dizziness as he pulled off his cowboy hat and ran a frustrated hand through his dark blond hair.

Where she'd avoided taking a good look at him inside, she couldn't help but look now.

He wore a black T-shirt, faded jeans and a look that said he was royally pissed. Tension rolled off his body and his jaw clenched. A muscle ticked wildly near his left cheek. His eyes glittered dark green, so dark that they seemed almost black in the dim lighting.

Almost purple.

She blinked and the color faded.

Obviously a trick of the light or her own frantic mind. She was dizzy, not to mention pretty well pissed herself.

Planting her hands on her hips, she glared. "Just what do you think you're doing?"

He set the hat back on his head and inched closer, making her crane her neck to look at him. "You wanted a man to make the first move. Well I just made it."

"That's not what I was talking about."

His voice lowered a notch. "Wasn't it? You wanted a man to act on his feelings, to take the lead, to be so insane with lust that he can't keep his hands off you. Well, here you go."

Excitement bolted through her, followed by a rush of doubt because no way—no way in *hell*—was Dillon Cash really and truly coming on to her.

Sure, she looked really hot in a new outfit she'd picked up at the boutique, but she had a closet full of hot clothes and they'd never made a difference.

Deep down, she knew she was a fake. A fraud. The entire town knew it and he was no exception. She wasn't sexy enough for him to make the first move.

Not in the past few days when they'd been smack-dab in

the middle of the most provocative lessons. Not last night when she'd stripped off her clothes and dropped to her knees in front of him.

And not now while they were standing in the middle of a parking lot, the air stagnant with the smell of French fries and stale beer from a nearby Dumpster, the stark light from a bare bulb gleaming overhead.

It was her imagination. Wishful thinking. Desperate hormones.

She'd gotten a taste of the richest, most decadent sex of her life, and she couldn't help but want another.

She *knew* it.

At the same time, there was no denying the fierce gleam in his eyes or the fact that he'd physically picked her up in the middle of a crowded honky tonk, in front of God and half the town, or the fact that he was staring down at her now, his eyes blazing with jealousy and a hunger that kicked her in the chest and sent the air whooshing from her lungs.

She swallowed past a sudden lump in her throat. "What exactly are you trying to say?"

"This." And then his mouth swooped down and captured hers.

Meg's heart beat double-time, the sound thundering in her ears, drowning out her conscience and every reason why this couldn't be happening. Even more, why it shouldn't—they were friends and she could fall for him too easily. He would inevitably break her heart because he wasn't the least bit interested in anything more than sex, and she would wind up alone and broken.

Again.

She slid her arms around his neck, stopped thinking altogether and just *felt*. The purposeful slant of his lips. The tantalizing dance of his tongue. The strong splay of his hands at the base of her spine. The muscular wall of his chest crushing her breasts. The hardness of his thighs pressed flush against hers.

Yum.

The kiss was hot and wet and mesmerizing, and much too brief. The last thought struck as she felt every muscle in his body go rigid. She opened her eyes just as he tore his mouth from hers. His head jerked around, his gaze fierce and searching and—

Nuh, uh.

She blinked once, twice, but his gaze didn't cool. Rather, his eyes gleamed like hot twin coals. Bright and intense and bloodred.

Her heart pounded, echoing in her head, drowning out the *whoosh* of cars from the nearby interstate, the crack of pool balls from inside, the crunch of gravel from behind a nearby Buick.

Her mind stalled on the thought and her gaze swiveled in time to see a shadow scramble away from the car.

A growl vibrated the air and her attention shifted back to Dillon in time to see his lips draw back. His fangs glittered as he whirled—

No.

Shock hit her like a thunderbolt and she clamped her eyes shut. The air rushed from her lungs and every muscle in her body froze.

Wait a second, *wait a second.*

She'd either had too much to drink or not enough, because there was no way she'd just seen…that he actually had…that he was actually a…. *No.*

Denial rushed through her, followed by a wave of panic when she opened her eyes to see Dillon, fangs still bared, eyes flashing. He took one step toward the Buick and collapsed.

Her gaze shifted to the small dart that protruded between his shoulder blades. Her heart hit the brakes and skidded to a stop. Fear rushed through her, cold and biting, dousing the anxiety and disbelief, and galvanizing her into action.

Not fear for herself that told her to get the hell out of there while she still could. No, she felt fear for him, spurring her to drop to her knees and reach out to him.

Because vampire or not, Dillon Cash was still her friend.

And he'd just been shot.

Meg called Jake McCann instead of the paramedics.

While she wanted to believe that her mind had been playing

tricks on her, deep in her heart, she knew that what she'd seen had been all too real.

Something had happened to Dillon two months ago. Something that went beyond a little Internet research on sex appeal. He'd really and truly changed. Physically. Mentally. Emotionally.

A *vampire*.

As much as she wanted to dismiss the insane notion, she couldn't.

Because it didn't just stir a rush of seemingly impossible questions. Instead it answered the biggest one of all—namely, how Dillon Cash had gone from geek to god virtually overnight.

One day he'd been the most clueless computer nerd in town and the next he'd morphed into Mr. Sex Appeal. He'd turned his back on Meg, pulled away from his family and embraced a new set of friends—the owners of the town's one and only custom motorcycle shop.

Jake McCann and Garret Sawyer had moved to Skull Creek around the time Dillon had changed. The men hadn't been friends of a friend or cousins of a cousin. They'd simply shown up one day, leased and renovated a local gas station, and Skull Creek Choppers had been born. While they kept up the pretense of being run-of-the-mill entrepreneurs—they sponsored a local little league team and paid their monthly dues to the local chamber of commerce—they didn't blend in with the other townspeople. No Sunday picnics at the park, no frequenting the one and only grocery store in town, no occasional lunches at the local diner. Rather, they kept to themselves and burned the midnight oil at their shop.

They were strangers for the most part. Tall, dark, hunky strangers who shared the same telltale tattoos on their biceps.

If Meg had had any doubts that Jake McCann had something to do with Dillon's transformation, they disappeared when he arrived in record time, picked up Dillon as if he weighed little to nothing, loaded him in the back seat of a black SUV, motioned Meg in after him and headed in the opposite direction of the nearest hospital.

She lifted her gaze from the man whose head she cradled in her lap and caught Jake's stare in the rearview mirror. His eyes gleamed bright and knowing and the words were out before she could stop them. "You're a vampire, too, aren't you?"

He didn't answer her.

He didn't have to.

For a split second, reality struck and the incredulity of what she'd just said hit her.

A bona fide, Bella Lugosi, *Dark Shadows,* Anne Rice, blood-sucking *vampire.*

Her brain railed against the notion, but then her memory stirred and she saw Dillon looming over her, his mouth hinting at the sexiest grin she'd ever seen, his eyes a bright, vivid blue. She remembered his pissed off look in the parking lot and the deep purple hue of his gaze.

A dozen other images rushed at her, pounding out the truth and fortifying it until it stared her in the face like a brick wall. Dillon showing up after sunset. Dillon appearing on her balcony. Dillon standing in front of her on the ledge at Cooter's Ridge. Dillon teasing and taunting and stirring her more than any other man in her past.

He'd done all of those things because he was more than a man.

"I know it's a little hard to believe," Jake said as if reading her thoughts. "I can't read them if you don't want me to," he added, sending a jolt of realization through Meg. "It's like closing the blind on a window. Nikki does it all the time."

Because Nikki knew the truth. And accepted it.

"She didn't at first. She didn't want to believe any more than you do. At the same time, she couldn't deny what was right in front of her." His gaze caught and held hers in the mirror. His eyes blazed as bright as the sun on a hot Texas day before cooling to a deep, fathomless blue. "Any more than you can."

"Maybe I'm hallucinating," she blurted, grasping for some plausible explanation.

"Does he feel like a hallucination?"

Her gaze dropped to the man stretched out on the seat next to her. She reached out, touching the tattoo that encircled one massive bicep. Warm skin met her fingertips as she traced the intricate pattern. Slowly. Carefully. Before easing to his chest. His heart beat a steady rhythm against her palm, answering one question but stirring a dozen more.

"We're susceptible to sunlight and garlic, a stake through the heart—the usual. We can't eat anything, but we can drink as much as we like. Though I don't usually advise it because we're very sensitive. We feel everything more strongly, more deeply than most, which makes us really cheap drunks. We have a reflection just like anyone else. We—"

"Could you just stop?" she blurted, her mind going into overload. Her temples throbbed and her forehead ached. It was all too much to grasp. "Please."

This was *not* happening. Not the bloodred eyes or the fangs or Dillon so limp and lifeless in her arms.

None of it.

Nada.

Zip.

It was all a bad dream brought on by too much stress and way too many Twinkies. Soon she would open her eyes, the sun would be shining and Dillon would be awake, his green eyes twinkling, his mouth crooked into a sexy grin.

"Don't worry," Jake's voice pushed past the frantic thoughts and she glanced up again. Her gaze locked with his and she saw the same flickering light she'd seen in Dillon's gaze so many times. "He isn't dead. Despite what most people believe, vampires are living and breathing creatures just like humans. We *are* humans." His gaze clouded. "Or we once were. Dillon is as alive as the next guy. More so now thanks to the blood flowing through his veins. My blood." An anguished light touched his gaze, dispelling yet another myth—that vampires were cold, ruthless creatures. "I had no choice. It was either turn him or let him die and I couldn't do that. He helped Nikki. He saved her. I had to return the favor."

As far out as it all seemed, her gut kept insisting otherwise and the words seemed to come despite her better judgment. "What exactly happened?"

"I…" He shook his head. "It's not my place to tell you." He shifted his attention back to the road. His hands tightened on the steering wheel as if he'd already said more than he meant to.

The rest would have to come from Dillon once he woke up.

If he woke up.

She forced aside the thought and the dozens of unanswered questions that raced through her mind. Resting her palm over the steady thud of his heart, she did the only thing she could think of at that moment—she prayed.

15

"DRINK."

The deep, familiar voice pushed into Dillon's head and peeled back the layers of darkness that smothered him.

He forced his eyes open. His head throbbed and the light hurt, seeming as if the drummer for Linkin' Park was playing a fast, furious solo in his skull. Pain gripped him like a vise, clamping tighter, building the pressure and urging him back toward oblivion.

The peace.

"Don't pass out on me now, buddy." A hand slid under Dillon's aching head and the hard edge of a glass pressed against his bone-dry lips.

The first few drops of intoxicating blood touched his tongue and his gut twisted. Then hunger took control. Where he hadn't been able to move a muscle just a moment ago, an instinct as primal as it was dangerous took over and he reached out. His mouth opened. His hands grasped the glass and he held on, gulping at the contents, eager for the life sliding down his throat.

"Easy, buddy. You'll make yourself sick drinking the bottled stuff so fast."

"More," Dillon groaned when he finished the last of the sweet, fortifying liquid.

His head dropped back to the pillow as he waited for Garret to refill the glass. He closed his eyes and relished the energy that pulsed from his stomach and spread through his limbs, firing his nerves and dispelling the last paralyzing shreds.

His heart sped, beating a fast, furious rhythm as he started to think.

To remember.

The images started at the club. He heard the music and smelled the cigarette smoke and he saw the woman standing across the room—

"Shit." The word burst past his lips as he bolted upright. His gaze skittered around the familiar room where he'd spent each day for the past few months. The recliner in the corner. The big-screen TV. The infamous bed with it's carved notches in the headboard.

There was no one sitting at the table or perched in the recliner or pacing a hole in the rug near his bed.

No one except Garret who sat on the edge of the mattress, an expectant look on his face, as he waited for Dillon to say something.

He couldn't. He couldn't think past the kiss and the pain and Meg staring at him as if he'd grown two heads. Or a very lethal looking pair of fangs.

Shit.

His gut twisted, a feeling that had nothing to do with the hunger and everything to do with the fact that she knew.

She knew.

Panic crashed over him, followed by a douse of anxiety and the desperate need to talk to her. *Now*. He started to move and a white-hot pain knifed between his shoulders blades. A groan ripped from his throat as he fell back to the bed.

"Take it easy. It's only been a few hours. You haven't had a chance to heal."

"What happened?" he finally managed to ask once the fire had died enough for him to think again. He took the refill Garret handed him and downed a huge gulp. "I was shot, wasn't I?"

Garret nodded. "But not with a bullet. Someone took you out with this." He held up a small dart. "It's a tranquilizer dart. The kind they use on animals. One shot and you can't move a lick. You've been sedated for the past three hours, your muscles paralyzed. It's starting to wear off, but it's going to take more time.

More sleep. And more blood." Garret held up the glass. "You can rely on this stuff, but it'll take longer to recover. If you want to heal quickly, you need the real thing."

He needed her.

The thought struck. A crazy, insane thought because Meg Sweeney was probably barricading her door at that very moment, hanging strands of garlic around the house and crossing herself sixty ways to Sunday.

She'd seen the truth for herself. He hadn't gone from the town geek to one of the hottest guys around. No, he'd gone from a town geek to a hot vampire, a round-trip ticket that would eventually bring him right back to where he'd started.

To being clueless and geeky and completely in love.

Love?

He wasn't in love with Meg. He liked her, of course. A helluva lot. She was his buddy. His pal. His *friend*.

The words were meant to reassure, but damned if they didn't make him that much more miserable.

"How did I get here?" he blurted, eager to ignore the rush of feelings that pushed and pulled inside of him.

"Meg called Jake and he picked you up. He called me on my cell—I was out—and I met you guys here. He went to pick up Nikki and the two of them waited around awhile before I finally convinced them that you were going to be okay. Actually, Jake knew it from the get-go, but Nikki wasn't buying it. She really cares about you." He shook his head as if the very thought puzzled the hell out of him.

As if Garret had seen far too much fear and revulsion in his two-hundred-plus years and couldn't grasp the concept of love and acceptance.

He couldn't and Dillon didn't blame him. Nikki was obviously the exception to the rule.

"Who shot me?" Dillon asked, his throat suddenly tight.

"You tell me." Garret leveled a stare at him. "Didn't you see someone? *Sense* them?"

"I…" The kiss rushed at him, the warm, sensuous lips eating at his, the lush body pressed to his, the sweet scent of strawberries and warm woman filling his nostrils, the soft, familiar gasps echoing in his head.

He'd sensed someone, all right.

"You went back for seconds, didn't you?" Garret asked.

"No." *Not yet.*

Not ever.

Because Meg was surely too scared to want him now. Unless Jake had mesmerized her. Vampires could look into a human's eyes and entrance them. It was a survival skill that helped them keep such a low profile. If someone saw too much, a vampire could easily erase their short-term memory. Like turning back the hands of a clock, Jake could have made Meg forget all that had happened in the past few days—Dillon's transformation in the parking lot, the kiss right before it, the sex the night before that.

That notion bothered him almost as much as the possibility that she feared him.

His body tensed and suddenly he needed to move. He forced himself upright, pushing his back up against the headboard. The movement brought with it a sharp pain between his shoulder blades and he winced.

Garret didn't say a word. He simply stared at Dillon, as if he could see the turmoil coiling inside of him.

As if Garret knew what haunted him—the fear of the past, of the future—because he dealt with similar demons.

The older vampire opened his mouth to say something, but then he seemed to think better of it. "You haven't been feeding properly," he finally murmured, killing the notion and shifting the subject away from Meg. "You're weak. It's no wonder whoever it was got the jump on you. You're lucky they didn't kill you."

"Why didn't they?"

"I haven't figured that one out. Obviously, we're not looking at a groupie. I've had women come after me before—" he winked

"—but they're usually tossing panties my way, not darts. A groupie wants to nail you, sure enough, but not like that."

"A vampire hunter?"

"I suppose it's possible." Garret shrugged. "But if it was, why didn't they stake you when they had the chance."

Because of Meg.

That's what he wanted to believe.

But Dillon knew enough about hunters to know that they were thorough. They saw vampires as the enemy and didn't mind killing a few innocents to further their cause. Meg's presence wouldn't have swayed them. They would have simply killed her, too.

"It's the Ancient One." Dillon voiced the one thought that niggled at him. "He knows we're out to get him, so he came to get us first."

"That still brings us back to the same question—why didn't he destroy you when he had the chance?"

"Maybe it was a warning. To let us know that he's on to us, that we'd better back off."

"Why not cut your head off and be done with it?"

"Because…" Dillon's mind raced. "I don't know. Maybe he likes playing games. Maybe that's what this is."

"Maybe." Garret seemed to think before shaking his head. "Go back to the blog tomorrow. Post again and then follow up on those leads. Get addresses to go with the names and then we'll take a little trip."

But they wouldn't have to. Dillon knew it, even if Garret wasn't half as convinced.

"If he was trying to warn us," Garret continued, "and we keep pushing, he'll be back. In the meantime—" he set the dart on the nightstand and pushed to his feet "—you need to sleep. I'll switch on the alarm system on my way out."

"So we just sit and wait for him to come after us? Shouldn't we do something?"

"You are doing something. You're healing."

Dillon rested a hand over his eyes to block out the faint glare. The movement sliced through him and he gasped.

"You're not in any shape to go searching for an ancient vampire who'll surely kick your ass before you can blink. Pain is a distraction."

One he desperately needed. He forced his legs over the edge of the bed and pushed to his feet. The pressure cut through him, ripping as he staggered to his feet. He focused on the sensation, letting the pain clear his head and force aside the worry and regret eating away at him.

"You really should stay in bed."

"I want to go to the shop." He paced toward the TV, his steps picking up the more he moved. He turned and walked back toward Garret. "I'm fine."

"You're not fine. You're hungry and unless you're going to go out and find a nice young redhead to sink your teeth into, then you might as well settle your ass back down and wait for the bottled stuff to kick in." When Dillon didn't immediately head for the door, Garret gave him a knowing look. "I'll bring your files back here." He motioned to the laptop sitting on a desk in the far corner. "You can work tomorrow."

"I can't just sit here and wait." Dillon turned and limped toward the TV again. *And think.*

"There are other options to pass the time."

"Yeah," he muttered, casting a sullen glance at the computer. "There's always solitaire."

"I actually prefer poker myself." The soft voice slid into his ears and Dillon's heart lurched.

It couldn't be.

That's what he told himself, but there was no denying the sweet scent of strawberries that filled his head and the frantic heartbeat that echoed in his ears.

His chest hitched and every nerve in his body tensed. He turned. And sure enough, there stood Meg.

16

"SO THIS IS WHERE YOU'VE been hiding out for the past few months." Meg swept a glance around the large, sprawling room, from a small sitting area complete with black leather recliner, chrome-and-glass coffee table and a big-screen TV, to a small oak table and chairs. An antique four-poster bed covered with lots of pillows and a down comforter dominated half the space. Soft rugs accented the hardwood floor and softened the otherwise masculine room. It looked like the typical man's apartment.

But Dillon Cash was far from typical.

Her gaze riveted on the nightstand and the small glass that held a quarter inch of dark red liquid. "So, you got all your sexy new moves from Internet research?" She shook her head and shifted her attention to the man who stood a few feet away. "I should have known there was more to it."

He still wore the same jeans he'd had on earlier, but he'd shed his shirt and boots. His chest was broad and bare. Gold hair sprinkled from nipple to nipple before narrowing into a thin line that bisected his six-pack abs. The soft silk circled his belly button before disappearing beneath the button fly of his jeans.

Her mouth went suddenly dry and she swallowed.

"You can find out anything online these days." He shrugged and the tattoos that circled his biceps flexed. "Why not sex appeal?"

"Because if it were that simple, I would have done it myself." Her gaze collided with his. "Why didn't you tell me the truth?"

"You wouldn't have believed me." He turned and walked a

few steps, pacing back and forth like a caged animal. "I had a hard enough time believing it myself."

"Actually, it's the one thing I would have believed. I've tried everything to change this town's perception, and you come along and do it just like that. The people here are set in their ways. It would take something phenomenal to open their eyes." A rip in the upper left thigh of his jeans played peekaboo with each step and gave her a glimpse of one hair-roughened thigh.

"So," she continued, her voice suddenly tight. "You really feed off of blood *and* sex?"

He nodded. "Sex more than the blood."

In her mind's eye, she saw him. He stood half-naked, towering over her. His penis, thick and ripe and proud, filled her hands.

"When a woman has an orgasm, it stirs the most delicious energy. I soak it up and it sates the bloodlust. For a little while, anyway."

"What about your own orgasm? Don't you have to…" She licked her lips, trying to force the image aside and quell the sudden butterflies in her stomach. "Don't you need to…" *He-llo? You're a grown woman. Just say the word.*

"Ejaculate?" His green eyes glittered with a knowing light. "It's not about my pleasure. It's about pleasuring someone else. If they get off, then I get off." His gaze drilled into hers, so deep and probing.

She shifted her attention to the massive headboard and the tell-tale notches. Curiosity washed through her, followed by a stab of jealousy. The words were out before she could stop them. "How many women have you actually slept with since the change?"

"The bed used to belong to Bobby McGuire. I bought it when they auctioned it off a few years back. Those notches are his. Impressive, huh?"

"If you're a fourteen-year-old boy who's just hit puberty." Her gaze shifted back to him. "So you haven't been keeping track the past few months?"

His green eyes twinkled. "I didn't say that."

"Then how many?" she pressed.

"Enough." He eyed her for a long moment, as if trying to decide what to tell her. Or what *not* to tell her. "But not here." His gaze darkened. "You're the first woman who's been here."

She ignored a sudden rush of joy and focused on the one question still burning inside of her.

He arched an eyebrow at her. "Only one?" he asked as if reading her thoughts.

He *was* reading them, she reminded herself.

He was a *vampire*.

He saw everything she saw, felt everything she felt. More so now that they'd had sex.

"Jake and Nikki filled me in on almost everything," she said, eager to ignore the sudden alarm bells that sounded and the small voice that whispered for her to turn and leave now. Before the bond grew even stronger. *Unbreakable*. "I know all the basics— no sunlight or garlic or wooden stakes. I also know that you can move faster than Margie Pinkerton at an all-you-can-eat buffet, and levitate and read minds. Your eyes change color depending on what mood you're in. You can even mesmerize someone and make them forget certain things if you want to."

"If they want to," he added. "While I can be persuasive, I can't override free will. Not if it's strong enough."

"I also know about the Ancient One, and how killing him will reverse the curse for all three of you." She licked her lips. "I know *how* you've changed, but I don't know about the change itself. The turning. What happened?"

"All vampires have a homing instinct that calls them back to the exact spot they were turned on the yearly anniversary of their turning. Once there, they relive those few moments where life and death collided. They feel the same pain and anguish. The same hunger. It can be overwhelming." He raked a hand through his hair. "You go a little crazy. Garret was in the middle of re-living his turning when I arrived on the scene. To make a long story short, I thought Nikki was in danger and I stepped in to protect her. Jake and I were facing off when Garret lost it. He went for my throat. I was dying, but then Jake offered me his blood." He shrugged again. "And here I am."

"You really tried to save Nikki?"

A grin crooked his lips. "Me and my Phillips screwdriver."

"That itty bitty thing you used to carry in your pocket?"

"The one and only."

She couldn't help but smile and for a few heartbeats, the tension between them seemed to ease.

"That was really brave," she said after a long moment.

A gleam lit his eyes and she had the inexplicable feeling that her opinion mattered a lot more to him than he wanted to admit. "I did what I had to do. What any friend would have done." His gaze caught and held hers. "By the way, thanks for calling Jake tonight."

She shrugged. "I did what any friend would have done."

The silence ticked by before his deep voice slid into her ears. "Is that why you're still here now?"

Her mind raced and she remembered the fear that had gripped her on the long ride to the ranch. She'd cradled his head and prayed for his safety. And she'd faced the truth—that she might never hear his voice again, or feel his touch or see his smile.

Tonight he'd been lucky.

But what about next time?

Someone was out there. A vampire hunter would surely come after Dillon again. And if it was the Ancient One himself? Then Dillon would go after him.

Either way, a confrontation was inevitable.

Meg had already lost one important person in her life. She wasn't adding her oldest and dearest friend to the list, not if she could do anything to help it.

It certainly wasn't because she wanted one more night with him.

This wasn't about sex. It was about being a friend.

It *was*.

She held tight to the thought and reached for the buttons on her vest.

"I'm here for this." She opened the garment and freed her

breasts. She wasn't wearing a bra tonight and the first whisper of air against her nipples brought them to throbbing awareness. The material slid off her shoulders and fell to the floor. "And this." She kicked off her boots and shed her socks. "And this." She hooked her fingers in the waistband of her jeans. She wiggled the denim down her hips and legs until the material pooled around her ankles and she stepped free. "And this," she said, finally shedding her lace thong.

Dillon fought the urge to pinch himself.

A dream, he told himself. This had to be a dream. No way would Meg willingly offer herself to him now that she knew the truth.

Yet here she was. Completely naked. Her full lips trembled and her eyes blazed with desire.

Because she knew the truth.

Because Meg Sweeney was all about the big S. She'd built her life trying to be perceived as sexy. She longed for it. And, thanks to the turning, Dillon now represented everything that she wanted. He oozed sensuality and stirred the same in every woman he came into contact with.

Where she'd once been the ultimate challenge for him, he was now the ultimate challenge for her.

That's what his head told him.

But his heart… He couldn't shake the crazy notion that maybe she wanted more than his cock between her legs and his tongue down her throat.

That she wanted to give, as well as take.

He stared deep into her eyes, searching for the truth, and saw…

What the hell?

"Nikki told me how to protect my thoughts." Her gaze locked with his and sure enough, he saw nothing except his own lust glittering back at him. "A woman's entitled to her privacy." She gave him a small smile before the expression faded. "Nikki also said that the reason you got shot tonight was because you haven't been feeding properly. Your senses aren't as sharp as they should be." She stepped toward him, her breasts quivering with each step until she reached a point midway between them. He knew then that while she was offering herself to him in the most blatant way, she wanted him to make the same effort and meet her halfway. "Maybe we can do something about that."

He stiffened. "Get out of here," he said, his voice gruff. "Before you do something you'll regret."

Uncertainty creased her beautiful features before her mouth drew into a firm line. Her eyes narrowed and her look morphed into one of pure determination.

She drew a deep breath that flared her nostrils and lifted her luscious breasts. "You could go for the usual spot." Her fingers fluttered down the side of her creamy neck. "Or maybe you'd rather do it here." She touched the underside of one breast and traced her ripe nipple. "Then again, maybe you'd rather taste me here." A few tantalizing touches and she slid her palm down, over the soft skin of her abdomen, to the inside of one thigh. "Or—" her breath caught as she dipped a finger between her legs "—even here." A gasp bubbled past her full lips and his gut twisted.

"You don't know what you're asking for."

"I'm not asking for anything. I'm giving." The last word hitched as she slid another finger into her steamy heat.

In the blink of an eye, he pinned her to the nearest wall.

"What—" she gasped, but her startled expression quickly faded into one of pure excitement as she stared up into his eyes.

She wanted the vampire, all right. She wanted to walk on the wild side, to unleash the beast inside of him, and suddenly that didn't seem like such a bad idea.

For all her boldness, she'd yet to see what he'd really and truly become. A glimpse would surely send her running even faster than that first horrible kiss back in the ninth grade.

"Or maybe I'll just try each spot until I find the one I like best," he growled, pulling back his lips. A hiss worked its way up his throat as he bared his fangs. His body trembled and he touched his mouth to her ripe throat.

She didn't stiffen when he rasped her soft flesh with the sharp edge of his incisors.

Rather, she arched her neck, the movement pushing her soft flesh against his fangs and pricking her skin. Her gasp sizzled in the air as a sweet drop of blood bubbled and slid down her neck.

Dillon caught it with his tongue, licking to the source and drawing another few sweet drops before lifting her. Her feet left the ground as he pushed her higher up the wall until her nipple brushed his lips.

Her breath caught as he latched onto the ripe tip and drew it deep. His fangs grazed the tender flesh around her areola and his groin tightened. Her nipple throbbed against his tongue as he sank into her just a hair and drew a few more drops of her delicious heat. The salty sweetness sent a dizzying rush to his head. His insides clenched.

More, more, more.

The chant echoed in his head and he pushed her higher, pinning her in place with his mind rather than his hands because he needed them now. He slid his palms around to cup her ass as he tilted her forward just a fraction and touched his lips to the slick flesh between her legs. He licked her then, tracing the seam with the very tip of his tongue before parting her.

She closed her eyes, her hands braced on his shoulders, her fingers digging into his flesh. Holding on.

Urging him on.

The thought pushed past the thunder of his own heart, making him all the more determined to give her what she thought she wanted and frighten her off for good. He drew her clit into his mouth and she jumped. He suckled her for a long moment before replacing his lips with his fingers, and shifting his mouth an inch to the side, to the tender flesh of her upper thigh. The smell of sex filled his nostrils and fanned his hunger into a living and breathing thing that overwhelmed him. A growl rumbled past his lips and he sank his fangs deep.

So deliciously *deep.*

Convulsions gripped her and she clutched at him.

A shudder ripped through him as he started to draw on her. Her delicious essence filled his mouth and the energy from her climax seeped into him at every point where flesh met flesh.

It was the ultimate in fulfillment for a vampire, and it wasn't nearly enough.

Not the warm, succulent body grasping at him, or the sweet essence pulsing in his mouth.

Dillon wanted more than just Meg's body and her blood.

He wanted her heart.

The realization sent a rush of determination through him and he stiffened. He fought the beast inside of him, urging it back down until he managed to draw back. Blood trickled from the spot and he lapped at it, licking at her wounds until they stopped bleeding.

And then he forgot all about driving her away, and decided to do his damnedest to get her to stay.

17

MEG WAS STILL REELING from the most mind-blowing orgasm of her life when she felt the soft mattress against her back. The bedsprings protested as Dillon pressed her down. Her eyelids fluttered open and she stared up at the man who loomed over her.

Straddling her, his knees trapping her thighs, he leaned back to gaze down at her. The single lamp that burned in the room was at his back, making him more shadow than man.

All except for his eyes.

She saw them clearly, glowing green fire that skimmed over her, setting her nerves ablaze and making her forget all about the exquisite pleasure they'd just shared. Hunger yawned and anxiety skimmed up and down her arms. She wanted more.

She wanted him.

And he wanted to put the brakes on. She felt the sudden shift in his mood even before he reached for her. It was there in the way he simply towered over and drank her in with his eyes. His hands clenched at his sides for several long seconds as he seemed to fight for control. After several heartbeats, he seemed to find it. Where they'd been fast and furious a moment before, the hands that reached for her now were slow and purposeful and oh so steady.

"I've pictured you like this so many times," he murmured, his voice thick and raw. "Beneath me, open for me, wet for me…" He skimmed her body, his fingertips brushing her neck, her collarbone, the slope of her breasts, the indentation of her ribs. "When I saw you that night from the balcony, I could hardly stand it. I wanted to rush in, throw the damned bottle to the wall and pleasure you myself."

But he hadn't. Because he couldn't. She hadn't invited him into her house at that point and, therefore, he'd been stuck in her doorway, waiting, watching. *Wanting*. The truth burned in the brightness of his eyes as they deepened and shifted until they burned a rich, vibrant purple. She wondered at the change in color.

"It's because I'm turned on," he murmured and she realized her thoughts were wide-open to him again.

She tried to block him, to focus her attention on shutting herself off mentally just as Nikki had said. But then he leaned down and flicked the tip of her nipple with his tongue and she forgot everything except the sharp sensation that knifed through her.

The ripe nub responded, hardening and throbbing, begging for more than the one decadent lick.

More.

She wanted him naked and hard and inside of her. Now.

Forever.

Hardly. This wasn't about tomorrow. It was about right now. About being a friend and helping him when he needed her most. It was about now. Anxiety rushed through her and she reached for him.

He caught her hands with one of his own and forced them up above her head to the headboard.

"Easy," he murmured, his other hand going to her abdomen. "We've got all night." He traced lazy circles, touching, relishing as if he'd never felt anything as soft as her skin.

Then he lowered his head and drew her nipple fully into the moist heat of his mouth.

Meg clenched her fingers, pushing against the hand that constrained her. She wanted to touch him. To feel him. To push things back up to the frenzied pace of a moment before so she didn't have to think about what he was doing to her. And *why*.

Why the slower pace and the forbidden words and the sudden determination that coiled his body tight and held every muscle in check.

The questions pushed and pulled, warring with the delicious heat that simmered through her as he licked a path across her skin to coax the other breast in the same torturous manner.

She rotated her pelvis, rubbing against his chest. She wanted him, surrounding her, consuming her, filling up the emptiness inside her once and for all.

Forever.

The thought struck again and she fought hard, her legs parting and her body bucking, but she was little match for his strength.

He suckled her again, so long and deep and *ahhh*...

One rough fingertip traced the soft folds between her legs, pushing inside just a delicious fraction that made her quiver and gasp. He lingered, suckling her breasts, first one then the other. Back and forth. Over and over.

She clenched and unclenched around the tip of his finger, trying to draw him deeper, but he didn't budge. Not until she was panting and whimpering and so desperate that she thought—no, she *knew*—she would surely die if he didn't do something.

Dillon smiled, his teeth a startling break in the black shadow of his face. Then the expression faded as he gazed down at her. His attention shifted, traveling from her face, down the column of her neck to her breasts, to the spread of her thighs and his finger, which poised at her pulsing cleft.

He pushed all the way in and she moaned, coming up off the bed as pure pleasure pierced her brain. The feeling, so consuming and exquisite, sucked the air from her lungs and she stopped breathing for a long moment. He didn't move, just held himself deep inside as her body settled around him and clamped tighter.

"I want you more than I've ever wanted any woman before," his voice was gruff. *Or after*.

The words sounded so clear and distinct in her head, as if he spoke them directly into her ear. He didn't. He didn't have to. He'd invaded her mind as well as her body, and they were telepathically linked now.

An unbreakable bond.

A spurt of excitement went through her, followed by a wave of anxiety that gripped her and refused to let go. She lifted her pelvis, focusing on the pleasure that gripped her as she worked her body around his decadent finger. She leaned into him only to pull away. She swayed from side to side, her movements frantic, desperate, as she pushed herself higher and higher, desperate to feel rather than think.

"You're so beautiful." The words pierced the humming in her ears and she went still. Her eyes opened to find him staring down at her. "The most beautiful woman I've ever seen." He kissed her softly on her swollen lips. "Or touched." He kissed her again. "Or loved."

Before the words could register, his mouth swooped down and captured hers in a deep kiss that went way beyond the sweet press of his lips. He coaxed her open and slid his tongue inside and drew on her sweetly, tenderly for several long moments. Until her frantic heartbeat eased and she forgot all about sucking him deeper into her greedy body. Instead, she wanted to wrap her arms around him, pull him even closer and feel his heartbeat against her own.

A second later, she found herself free to do just that.

Her hands slid over his shoulders and held tight. She relished the feel of his body as it pressed against hers, his heartbeat so steady and sure against her breasts. She'd never felt closer to a man at that moment.

A vampire.

She tried to remember that all-important fact. It explained the sudden about-face and the fact that he couldn't keep his hands off of her and that they were having the hottest, most passionate sex of her entire life.

Because he was a vampire.

She could have been any woman, she knew. But damned if he didn't make her feel like the only woman.

His woman.

A trick of the trade, she told herself. Vampires could mesmerize. She'd learned that tonight. Dillon was just playing mind games.

And doing it quite well.

He canted his head to the side and deepened the kiss. He plundered her mouth with his, exploring and savoring. The air stalled in her lungs and her heart sped faster. A few more seconds and he tore his mouth from hers.

He slid down her body, now slick from the fever that raged inside of her, and left a blazing path with the velvet tip of his tongue. With a gentle pressure, he parted her thighs. Almost reverently, he stroked the soft, slick folds between her legs.

She was wet and throbbing and he swore softly. Tremors seized her when she felt his warm breath blowing softly on the inside of her thigh, directly on the tiny prick points where he'd drunk from her. His tongue darted out, flicking first one then the other, and it was like being zapped by white lightning. Pleasure sliced through her, cracking her open from head to toe. She gasped and dug her nails into his shoulders as wave after wave of ecstasy washed through her.

She wasn't sure what happened after that. She was too busy floating, her body weightless, her mind buzzing with sensation. She only knew that one minute he had his jeans on and the next, he was settling his naked body between her damp thighs.

A condom.

The warning sounded in her head when she felt his hard, hot length rub her pulsing clit. She tried to clamp her legs shut, but he was too close, his thighs wedging her open. His deep voice whispered through her head.

I can't hurt you. I wouldn't hurt you.

The seconds ticked by as he waited for her. She finally nodded and it was all the encouragement he needed.

With a swift thrust of his hips, he impaled her on his rigid length and all worry faded as heat drenched her. Sensation overwhelmed her at first. The feel of him so hot and thick pulsing inside her nearly made her come without any warning.

She anchored her arms around his neck and her muscles clamped down around his erection. She didn't want to let him go, but he had other ideas.

He withdrew and slid back in for the second time. His hard length rasped her tender insides, creating a delicious friction that sent a dizzying rush straight to her brain. He pulled out again, and went back for a third time. A fourth.

His body pumped into hers over and over, pushing her higher with each delicious plunge. She lifted her hips, meeting him thrust for thrust, eager to feel more of him. Harder. Deeper. Faster.

Look at me.

She opened her eyes and stared up at him as he poised over her. He pushed into her, his penis hot and twitching, and she knew it was his last and final time. He was going over the edge before her.

It's not about my own pleasure. It's about pleasuring someone else.

Yet here he was, mindless with pleasure, lost in his own orgasm.

His arms braced on either side of her, his muscles bulging and tight as he held himself. The tendons in his neck stood out. His eyes blazed a bright, vivid purple. His jaw clenched and his lips parted. His fangs gleamed as he let loose a loud hiss that faded into a long moan as Meg arched her pelvis.

His penis twitched and throbbed, and she felt a spurt of warmth. He bucked once, twice and she followed him over the edge. Convulsions gripped her body and suddenly she was floating again on a cloud of pure satisfaction.

Several breathless moments passed as she lay there, trying to come to grips with what had just happened.

He'd climaxed first.

This time, she reminded herself. But she'd come plenty of times before, when he'd had her pinned against the wall. He'd already drank his fill. Of her blood and her energy.

That's what she told herself because she certainly wasn't going to consider the alternative—that he might feel something more for her. Something that had nothing to do with being a vampire and everything to do with being a man.

A man in love.

Right.

Dillon Cash didn't love her. He couldn't love her. Because regardless of what had just happened—a fluke, of course—he *was* a vampire.

One who'd slept with a ridiculous number of women.

One who would sleep with even more.

He had to in order to survive. She wanted him to. That's why she'd offered herself to him tonight. Because he needed her.

Friends, she reminded herself.

But when Dillon rolled onto his back and pulled her flush on top of him, she felt like anything but his friend. His hands stroked her back, her buttocks, holding her close, touching her intimately. A lover's touch rather than a friend's.

The notion sent her scrambling from the bed.

"Meg?" His voice followed her as she snatched up her clothes. "What's wrong?"

"It's late," she blurted the first thing that popped into her head. "I need to get home." Dread welled inside of her and panic beat at her temples as she jerked on her vest and pants, her movements frantic and hurried. She needed to get out of here. *Now.* Before she did something she would surely regret.

Like climb back into bed with him and stay there forever.

"Wait!" His frantic voice followed her, his footsteps dogging her up the stairs to the ground floor. "Would you just wait a second?"

She rushed through the house, snatching up her purse as she headed for the front door.

"Dammit, woman!" He caught one hand while the other reached for the doorknob.

His fingers burned into hers and she yanked open the door. Early-morning light spilled through the open doorway. His hand fell away and a loud hiss sizzled in her ears. He murmured a fierce *shit* as he stumbled backward.

She barely resisted the urge to turn and reassure herself that he was okay.

He would be. She'd made sure of that tonight. She'd given him what he needed—her body and her blood—and that was more than enough to strengthen him against whatever he might face.

A vampire hunter. The Ancient One. A few rays of sunlight.

They were friends, she reminded herself, and then she stepped out into the morning sunlight, pulled out her cell phone and called Nikki for a ride home.

HE'D BEEN WRONG ABOUT her.

Dillon paced the floor in his room and ignored the exhaustion that tugged at his muscles. It was daylight and he needed to sleep. To rejuvenate.

Christ, he'd been wrong. So fucking *wrong*.

The truth crystallized as he stared at the tell-tale stain on his sheets from where he'd bitten her. His nostrils flared and his mouth watered. He could still taste her. Even more, he could feel her. The anguish that ate away at her. The uncertainty as she paced the front porch upstairs and waited for Nikki. The fear as she thought about going back inside to see him just one more time.

They were linked now and as much as that should have bothered him, it didn't.

He loved her. He always had, even way back when he'd been too young and naive to know it. And later when he'd been too damned uncertain to act on it.

And she loved him.

Man or vampire or both?

He didn't know, and he never would because he refused to take a chance.

That's why he'd convinced himself that her attraction wasn't to him, but to the sexy beast he'd become. Because deep down, beneath the confidence and charisma that came with being a vampire, he was still the same man. The same boy who'd acted on a whim so long ago and had ended up in the hospital.

He'd been scared to death ever since.

He'd blamed his parents for being overprotective and paranoid. But in reality, he'd been just as bad. Afraid to take chances, to live for the moment, to *live*, period.

Sure, he'd been burning the candle at both ends for the past two months, enough to break Bobby's record and go down in the history books, but that was different. Being a vampire reduced the risk. He knew no man could best him physically. And no woman could refuse him sexually.

No woman, that is, until Meg.

She'd held out at first and surprised the hell out of him.

He realized then that she wasn't just any woman.

She was every woman.

And she loved him even if she didn't want to admit it.

Right now, a voice whispered, taunting him as he collapsed on the bed and gave in to the darkness tugging and pulling at his senses. *At this moment. But later when things go back to normal?*

Maybe. Maybe not.

He didn't know. He only knew that it was a chance he was suddenly willing to take rather than face the thought of losing her completely.

For a lifetime.

Forever.

"LOOKS LIKE SOMEBODY HAD a busy night," Terry remarked when Meg walked into the boutique several hours later, after a half-hour ride back to town with Nikki and more than one knowing glance.

The woman hadn't said much when she'd dropped Meg off at home to check on Babe except "Don't worry. Everything will be okay."

The only trouble was, Meg couldn't shake the feeling that from this moment on, nothing would be okay. Her life had changed tonight. He'd changed.

And there would be no going back to the way things had been.

She ignored the crazy thought. Everything would be okay. Dillon was stronger now. Together, he and Jake and Garret would find and defeat the Ancient One. He would reclaim his humanity, go back to being her good buddy, and all would be right with the world.

All she had to do was keep her distance from now on until he was back to his old self—and not nearly as tempting—and everything *would* be okay.

She clung to the notion and focused on Terry. "Don't tell me—you hooked up with some hot and hunky cowboy and had wild and uncontrollable sex last night."

"Not me," the woman blurted. "You." Terry handed over the Lifestyle section from the morning's issue of the *Skull Creek Gazette*. "You made Tilly's *Around the Town* column!"

Meg unfolded the paper and stared at a picture that had been taken at The Roundup last night. She and Colt stood wrapped in a heated embrace, right above the caption *There's a new sheriff in town!*

She skimmed the three paragraphs about the town's hottest new real estate agent who seemed a shoe-in to unseat one of the regulars and make next week's Randiest Roosters list.

Oddly enough, Meg didn't feel half as disappointed as she should have over the fact that she didn't get so much as a mention. Instead, she skimmed the background faces, searching for one in particular.

She caught a glimpse of Dillon near the bar, his gaze trained on her. A very vivid image of last night rushed at her and she remembered his blond head between her legs, his mouth drawing on her tender flesh, and the rush of pleasure she'd felt.

He hadn't just taken from her. Rather, as her essence had flowed into his mouth, she'd felt something flow back—a fierce current that had pulsed from his body into hers, pulling them closer, winding them tighter, *connecting* them.

No.

He'd fed and she'd eased her conscience knowing that she'd done everything possible to help him in the battle that awaited him. Now it was back to work.

To life.

Bye-bye Jezebel.

Her gaze dropped to the article again. Not one mention of her. Or her sexy outfit or the fact that Colt hadn't been able to keep his hands off her.

Nothing.

She waited for the rush of disappointment, the clenching in her gut, the dread in her stomach and the certainty that her tombstone would one day read:

Here lies tough and rough Manhandler Meg,
Who loved sports and kicked ass and could drain a keg,
She tried shedding her image, but was still a bruiser,
Now she's six feet under and a perpetual loser.

But when she drank in the page, the only thing she felt was a strange tightening in her chest. Her gaze kept going back to Dillon and the dark look on his face.

As if he felt more for her than just a vampire's lust.

She remembered last night and the soft mattress at her back, the strong, purposeful lover leaning over her, the strange gleam in his eyes as he'd stared down at her.

A look that had had nothing to do with the fact that he wanted her and everything to do with the fact that *he* wanted *her*.

"Are you okay?" Terry's voice drew her back to reality.

"Fine." Meg shook away the haunting images. She drew a deep breath and swallowed past the sudden lump in her throat. "Why?"

"For a second there, you looked like you were going to cry."

"Cry?" She forced a laugh. "Why would I do something ridiculous like that?"

Because you love him, stupid. You. Love. Him.

Hardly. She liked him. A lot. They were the best of friends. But honeymoon-in-Jamaica, house-in-the-suburbs, kids-and-a-minivan, 'til-death-do-us-part *love?*

Love was the culmination of everything—admiration, respect,

comfort, protection, rip-off-your-clothes-and-get-naked-now-desperation, trust—the entire cake so to speak, complete with a layer of filling and sprinkles on top.

Meg was only interested in the butter-cream icing. The rich, decadent, addictive lust. She wanted to feel desired, sought after, *wanted*.

All the things Dillon had made her feel last night, and then some.

"Good," Terry said, drawing Meg's attention before she could dwell on the last thought. "Because one depressed woman around here is enough."

Meg took a good look at her assistant and noted the dark circles under the woman's eyes. "You look terrible."

"The end result of zero sleep and a gallon of Rocky Road ice cream."

"You ate an entire *gallon?*"

"Hank called. And called. And a little after midnight, he showed up."

"Don't tell me you slept with him again?"

"If I had, I wouldn't have needed the ice cream." She stiffened. "I stood strong, told him to get lost and then slammed the door in his face. And then I headed for the fridge."

"What did he do?"

"Nothing. He sat on my front steps for a little while and then he left. Then he came back and sat a while longer. Then he left. Then he came back. It was that way all night. I snuck out this morning as soon as he left for the eighth time."

"You should have called the police."

"Maybe." She shrugged. "But I feel responsible. I'm the one who let him back into my life." She shook her head. "I can't believe I slept with him. I mean, I know why I did it. The sex was always really great between us and I haven't actually had sex in a really long time, and so when I saw him, I couldn't help myself. But I knew it was the wrong thing and I did it anyway. What was I thinking?"

The same thing Meg had been thinking when she'd offered

her body and her blood to Dillon Cash—that she could handle it. That she could give herself to him and then walk away.

Forget.

If only she could.

"I'm so stupid."

"Aren't we all?" Meg ignored Terry's questioning look. "There's no use beating yourself up. Get over it. Move on. Have your phone number changed and if he shows up again, call the police."

Terry looked hesitant, but then she seemed to gather her courage. "Okay." She nodded and her determination seemed to deflate just a little. "I wish I knew what it is about this guy that makes me stop thinking like a sane rational adult."

"He's good in bed."

That was it. That was the only reason Meg Sweeney was thinking such crazy thoughts about love and marriage and happily-ever-after with a man like Dillon Cash. A *vampire*. He was the first to make her feel like a vibrant, sexy woman. Of course, she would feel more than friendship for him.

More, as in gratitude. Concern. And, of course, lust. He was hot and sexy. It only made sense that she would want him more than her next breath.

And fear. Not of him, but for him. She still couldn't shake the tightening in her chest when she'd seen him hit the ground last night or the all-important fact that he was still in danger.

Someone was still out there and it was just a matter of time before something happened.

A strange melancholy wrapped around her. She set aside the newspaper. "We should get going. We've got a busy Saturday ahead of us."

Terry nodded, gathered her composure and headed into the front part of the store to unlock the front door. Meanwhile, Meg sat down at her computer, determined to get a stack of orders finished before her first fitting.

She did her best to ignore the doom that settled in her gut and told her today was going to be the worst day of her life.

Impossible.

That day had already come and gone a long time ago and Meg wasn't ready for a repeat.

Not now. Not ever.

18

IT WASN'T THE WORST DAY of her life, but it was close.

Meg came to that realization as the hours passed and things seemed to go from bad to *really* bad.

First she discovered that the new seamstress she'd hired had eloped to Las Vegas. The woman had taken Chantal Mortimer's twenty-fifth anniversary dress for a simple hem three days ago. That morning, she'd appeared in the wedding announcements section of the *Skull Creek Gazette* wearing said dress and a wedding ring the size of a small third world country. Chantal had been furious—and jealous because her own ring weighed in at a whopping half carat less—and had demanded her money back. Meg had given her a prompt refund, only to have the woman rant for a full hour before she'd headed over to the diner for a complimentary lunch courtesy of the boutique.

Then Margie Westbury arrived. Margie had ripped her dress for tonight's banquet at the Elks lodge and now needed a new one, which wouldn't have been a problem had she not been a size twenty-eight special order. Tammy Greenburg wanted a one-of-a-kind sequined number she'd seen on CMT and couldn't understand why Meg didn't stock oodles of them (ahem—they call them one-of-a-kind for a reason). Sue Carrigan had gained twenty pounds and couldn't fit into the wedding dress she was scheduled to wear in exactly one week. And Honey Harwell nixed all ten of the special order dresses Meg had had overnighted for her Saturday afternoon fitting.

Then Terry's ex showed up. Not once, but five times.

And to make matters as bad as they could be, Meg couldn't stop thinking about Dillon.

Images played over and over in her mind. Memories. From when they'd been kids and he'd taught her to play chess and boot up her computer. Last Christmas when he'd handed over a new collar for Babe and a matching leash. The night at the motel when she'd seen him up close and personal for the first time since the turning. She'd gotten her first dose of pure, unadulterated lust then and she'd been craving it ever since.

Add a wonderful friendship to the overwhelming emotion, and it was no wonder she felt so mixed up inside. So drawn to him. That, and the fact that they were truly linked now that he'd drunk from her.

She could feel him, smell him, sense him.

Sensations that grew stronger once the sun dipped below the horizon and dusk settled over the town.

She knew the moment he opened his eyes. She felt the steady beat of his heart, the jump of his pulse and the power that lived and breathed inside of him. She even felt his determination.

Dillon Cash was coming for her.

Her pulse leapt and for a split second, she felt a rush of excitement. He was the first man to really and truly sweep her off her feet. The first to go nuts and ravish her. Her fantasy come to life.

It wasn't the man himself that made her heart beat faster.

No, it was the idea of him.

That's the conclusion Meg finally came to as the day faded into evening. She fought down a wave of nerves and picked her way through the front of the store, snatching up anything even close to Honey's size. The girl was still there, planted in a chair in the main dressing room, her iPod blaring as she waited for Meg to return with more choices.

Meg added a crimson-colored shift to her already overflowing arms and then turned to yet another rack. Her thighs touched and rubbed. Flesh grazed the twin prickpoints and desire knifed through her, sharp and fierce. Her legs trembled and her breath caught, and the dread churned deep inside of her.

Because the more turned on she was, the harder it would be to resist him.

She would resist. She didn't want to lose him as a friend.

That's what would happen. Romantic entanglements were fleeting. She knew that firsthand.

If she acted on the crazy lust burning her up from the inside out, she would enjoy herself for a little while. Maybe even a long while. But eventually Dillon would move on to another woman, or morph back into his old self and lose the desire for her that he felt right now. Either way, the fire would die, and so would their friendship.

She wasn't going to let that happen.

He'd been the one constant in her life over the past few years. The one person she'd always been able to count on. She didn't want to lose that.

She wouldn't.

Which was why when he showed up, *if* he showed up, she would simply set him straight and tell him the truth—while she really enjoyed the sex, she didn't have any romantic feelings for him and so it was best that they stop pretending and go back to being friends.

Her skin prickled as she retrieved the last dress and turned toward the dressing room. Awareness skittered up and down her spine.

He was coming, all right.

Good. The sooner she set the record straight, the sooner she could salvage their friendship.

If only she didn't get the sinking feeling that it was already too late.

TONIGHT WAS THE NIGHT.

Dillon stepped out of the shower and reached for a towel.

He was going to put it all on the line and pour out his heart.

Meg would listen, throw her arms around him and everything would be okay.

Or not.

He ignored the doubt, pulled on his clothes and snatched up his keys. It was early in the evening and Garret was still downstairs in his own apartment. Probably getting ready to go out and feed.

His own stomach grumbled as he bypassed the fridge—and the blood. But he'd had enough last night to last him awhile. He felt strong, his senses alert, his nerves alive. No, what he wanted now had nothing to do with the crimson heat flowing through her veins. He wanted more this time. *Everything.*

He spent the next ten minutes punching his way through security codes. Meg hadn't dealt with the same when she'd fled that morning because the alarm had been on a timer that hadn't kicked on until 9:00 a.m. Otherwise, she would have set off a world of noise when she'd hightailed it and ran.

She was still running, but not for long. Dillon intended to catch her and talk some sense into her. They could make it. Jake and Nikki were proof.

But Nikki loves Jake.

Meg loved Dillon, too. He knew it. He felt it. She was just too stubborn to admit it. But now was not the time to be ornery. Not with the rest of their lives at stake.

Fifty or so years if his instincts were correct and the Ancient One was close.

Forever if not.

He didn't know, he just knew that however long he had, he wanted to spend it with Meg Sweeney. Starting tonight.

He climbed onto his motorcycle and gunned the engine.

But first, he had something to take care of.

"DROP THE MACE, MOM," Dillon said a half-hour later as he stood in the front yard of his house and felt the woman who'd come up behind him.

In the blink of an eye, he whirled and faced her. She wore a black bodysuit, a determined expression and enough bug spray to kill every mosquito in Texas. And in her hand, she was holding the biggest can of Mace he'd ever seen. His gaze shifted to the second figure. His dad reeked of bug spray, as well. He also wore the same black bodysuit, as well as a mask. Thick bifocals perched on his nose and covered the eyeholes of the black knit. He clasped a stun gun in one hand and a net in the other.

But the older man wasn't the threat right now.

No, the tension washed off his mother in huge waves. She was worried and scared and she wasn't backing down until she had Dillon hog-tied in her tent.

"It's for your own good, baby," she told him, taking a tentative step forward. "They've brainwashed you and it's up to us to rewire you."

"I promise. I'm not brainwashed."

"Of course you don't think so. No one who's brainwashed ever thinks that they are. That's what makes it so obvious that you're under their spell. Who is it? Those Moonies? A satanic cult? That group I saw on *CNN* that worships Krispy Kreme donuts? I knew I should have let you have donuts as a child. Then you wouldn't have been so anxious to run out and get your sugar high somewhere else." Anguish fueled her voice. "But I was trying to protect you. Really I was."

"I know." His own voice was smooth and calm, a direct contrast to the nervousness raging inside him. He felt as if he were a child all over again, showing his mother his infected cut, disappointing her. "You didn't do anything wrong. You did a good job raising me."

"I failed. Not once, but twice. No more." She stiffened, taking another step toward him. "I'm doing my duty now. I'm saving my baby." Another step and her finger went to the spray trigger.

"Drop. The. Mace." He stared deep into her eyes and said it once more. He didn't want to push her too hard. He wanted her conscious for this.

At the same time, if he didn't resort to a little mind over matter, he was going to find himself hog-tied, hanging upside down in a nearby tent, his mom stuffing Krispy Kreme's donuts down his throat before he could get a word in edgewise.

Her mouth dropped open and her hand went slack. A glazed look came over her and the can clattered to the ground.

He turned to his father, but the man wasn't staring at him as if he'd grown two heads. No, he was staring at his wife's catatonic body.

"Just put the stun gun away," Dillon told his father, but the older man had already stuffed it into his pocket.

"I've been trying for years to get your mother to shut up like that." His father peeled off the mask he'd been wearing and eyeballed his son. "How'd you do that?"

"You really want to know?"

"Are you kidding?" A grin tugged at his father's mouth and genuine interest gleamed in his gaze.

The tension coiling in Dillon's gut eased just a little. Maybe telling them wasn't going to be as bad as he'd thought.

He spent the next half hour sitting on the front porch, filling his dad in on the specifics of what had happened to him while his mother sat in a small lounge chair, a passive look on her face.

Other than an initial rush of disbelief, his father didn't seem all that shocked. If anything, he looked somewhat relieved and Dillon found himself remembering what Meg had said about the truth being the only thing that made any real sense.

She'd obviously been right.

At least as far as his dad was concerned.

Dillon shifted his attention to his mother. While she hadn't been able to move, she'd heard every word. Dillon had made sure of that. He fought down his own fear, lifted the trancelike veil and waited for her reaction.

She took one look at him, let out a shriek and passed out cold.

It wasn't exactly the *"It's okay. I love you anyway, son,"* he'd been hoping for, but at least she hadn't gone into cardiac arrest.

"Give her some time," his father clapped him on the shoulder as he pushed to his feet.

"What about you? Are you all right with this?"

"I don't know." The man shrugged. "It's pretty unbelievable. At the same time, your mother's been living in a tent for three weeks straight now, so I'm not beyond buying the impossible." His gaze collided with Dillon's and worry lit his expression. "I just want you to be okay."

"I am."

"Good because I was afraid I was going to have to zap you with the stun gun. I still haven't figured out how to do it without goosing myself."

Dillon helped his father load his mother into the car for yet another trip to the E.R. for smelling salts. And possibly a mental evaluation should she start spouting off about the story he'd just told them.

But it was a chance he had to take. He was through playing it safe and worrying over each and every consequence. No more being scared.

No, he was facing his fears and acting on his feelings for the first time in his life.

He only hoped Meg was ready to do the same.

He fought down a rush of uncertainty, climbed onto his motorcycle and headed into town.

MEG IGNORED THE URGE to throw her hands into the air, or better yet, slide them around Honey Harwell's neck.

The young girl stood center stage in the back dressing room. It was almost seven and Elise had yet to return. Other than Terry and Hank who were once again having words in the back alley, Meg and Honey were all alone.

Meaning no one would hear if she decided to get physical. That, or wash the girl's smart mouth out with a little heavy-duty soap.

She resisted the appealing thought and summoned her patience. "Let's try this once again. It's the perfect cut and color."

"It sucks. It more than sucks. It royally sucks."

Where was a good bar of Ivory when she needed one?

Meg drew a deep breath and tried a different approach. "It

doesn't suck as much as the others, right? I mean, they sucked so bad they reeked," she reminded the girl of her earlier comments.

Honey seemed to think. "I hate this. I want to go home."

"Then try the dress on again because that's the only way you're getting out of here. Your mother said to pick something by the time she got back or she was taking your iPod."

"This bites," Honey breathed as reached for the dress.

Amen.

Meg pulled the curtains on the dressing room and debated whether or not to pick up the phone and call 911.

"…over, I'm telling you." Terry's voice carried from the partially open back door where she stood with Hank—again. "Can't you just leave me alone?"

"But I love you, baby. You mean the world to me. All those other women didn't mean crap."

"I don't care about them. That's the past. I've moved on. So should you."

"But you can't just make love to a man and then turn your back…"

Meg bypassed the phone and retrieved a small can of Mace she kept under her cash register. She'd promised Terry to let her handle Hank her own way. As long as he kept a mild tone of voice and didn't get physical, Meg intended to keep that promise. But at the first sign of real trouble, she was giving him a face full.

She was just about to head back into the dressing room to check on Honey when she heard the rumble of a motorcycle. She turned in time to see Dillon pull up to the curb in front of her shop and kill the engine. Muscles rippled and bunched as he climbed off the sleek black chopper.

Her heart shifted into overdrive as the bell on the front glass jingled.

He wore a pair of jeans and black T-shirt. His jaw was set, his face determined. Emotion blazed in the deep green depths of his eyes, so fierce and telling and—

No!

Panic bolted through her and she opened her mouth before he had the chance. "Don't say it."

"Don't say what?" He arched one blond brow and stepped toward her.

She took a step back. "Don't say what I think you're here to say."

"I told my folks."

"You'll just ruin everything," she rushed on before his words registered and she caught herself. "Come again?"

"I told them and they were okay with it." He shrugged. "At least my dad was. The verdict is still out on my mom. I realized something yesterday. For all my newfound boldness, I've still been holding back. Afraid." His eyes glittered with a knowing light. "Just like you."

Before she could blink, much less open her mouth and voice the denial that sprang to her lips, he was standing in front of her. Large, strong hands cradled her face. "Don't be scared."

He touched her so softly, so tenderly that her throat tightened. "I'm not afraid of you," she finally managed to whisper.

"No." He forced her gaze to meet his. "You're afraid of you."

His words sank in as he stared down at her, into her. He saw the frantic thoughts that raced through her head. The anxiety. The denial. The fear.

She fought against the notion and stumbled backwards, away from his warm hands and his probing stare. "I am *not.*"

"Yes, you are." He let his hands fall to his sides, but he didn't look the least bit happy about it. His fingers clenched and it was all he could do no to reach for her again. "You're afraid to let go, to fall in love, to *be* in love. Because if you don't put yourself out there, you can't get hurt." His gaze darkened and suddenly she saw herself sitting on the floor in the kitchen, Babe in her arms, the policeman lingering nearby. "If you don't have anything, then you can't lose it. That's why you're afraid of love."

Her throat constricted and a rush of tears burned the backs of her eyes. She blinked and fought for her voice. This was crazy. He was crazy. "I love a lot of things. Babe. My grandparents."

"You loved them *before* your father died. But since, you haven't let yourself get close—really close—to anyone. You're afraid, all right. Afraid to live, to love, to be yourself. That's why you've tried so hard to change all these years. You want to forget the woman you were, to bury the past."

"I wasn't a woman back then. I was a tomboy."

"You were a woman, all right. One hundred percent. And you could hold your own against any man. You still can. The difference is, you were comfortable in your own skin then and you're not now. Because being in that skin reminds you too much of your father, of your loss, of your pain." He reached for her again, his hands catching her shoulders, sliding up her neck, cradling her cheeks. "You have to let it go, baby. You can't keep running and hiding. Just let go."

She wanted to. She wanted to slide her arms around his neck and give in to the flood of emotion that threatened to blind her.

But she'd been holding back for so long, fighting so hard, that her instincts kicked in and she held tight to the denial racing through her. "You're crazy. You don't want to face the fact that I don't have feelings for you and so you're making all of this up to ease your wounded ego."

"If that's the truth, then look me in the eyes and tell me you don't have feelings for me," he countered. His hands splayed on either side of her face, anchoring her in place, forcing her to face him. To face herself. "Tell me you don't love me the way that I love you."

"I..." She tamped down on the anxiety pumping her heart faster and fought against the urge to turn her face into his palm, to kiss the throbbing pulse beat on the inside of his wrist, to lose herself in the man towering over her.

It would be so easy to give in.

To wind up on the floor, raw and open and heartbroken.

"I don't love you," she said, forcing the words out. And then she did what she should have done instead of propositioning him that night at the motel.

She turned her back on Dillon Cash and walked away.

DILLON BARELY RESISTED the urge to throw her over his shoulder, take her back to his place and love her until she stopped denying him and finally accepted the truth.

He wouldn't manhandle her because that's what she wanted—a convenient excuse to dismiss what she felt as lust.

But it was more, even if she refused to admit it.

He watched her disappear into the back and forced himself to turn. He pushed through the door and strode toward his motorcycle. He was about to climb on, to get the hell away before he buckled and gave in to the emotion welling inside of him, when he heard the raised voices coming from around back.

"…can't do this to me. Not again."

"Come on, Hank. Settle down."

"It's you who needs to settle the hell down. You can't play with a man's emotions like that."

It wasn't so much what the man said that distracted Dillon from his own damnable feelings and drew him around the side of the building. It was the threatening edge in his voice.

A few steps later, Dillon rounded the back of the boutique. His gaze sliced through the darkness in time to see the man reach for Meg's assistant.

In the blink of an eye, Dillon reached them. He caught one of the man's hands before it slid around the woman's throat.

"What the—"

"Leave her alone," Dillon cut in.

"Get lost," the man growled, pulling and tugging against Dillon's viselike grip. "This ain't none of your business. This is between me and my woman, here."

Dillon arched an eyebrow at Terry Hargove. Fear lit her eyes and she quickly shook her head.

"She's not your woman," Dillon told the man, squeezing

just enough to make his point. Bones cracked and the man shrieked. "Is she?"

"N-no," the man bit out when he finally seemed to find his voice.

"Good. Now get the hell out of here. And don't come back." Another squeeze and then he let go.

The man scrambled from the alleyway and Dillon turned back to the frightened woman. "You didn't see that," he told her. She looked startled at first, and then her body seemed to relax. Her eyes glazed over as she stared into his eyes. "Go back inside and forget what just happened. Forget about him."

She nodded and Dillon had half a mind to recruit Terry for his cause. A few persuasive thoughts and he could easily have the woman trying to convince Meg that he was the greatest thing in the world.

The trouble was, he wanted Meg to come to that conclusion herself.

To want him of her own free will.

To want him enough to admit it.

And so he tamped down his own desperation and watched Terry disappear through the back door. Hinges creaked and the lock clicked. He forced himself to turn away.

He'd risked it all and he'd lost.

The realization made his gut clench. Hopelessness rushed through him, so thick and consuming that he barely heard the footsteps behind him.

The sound pushed its way past the thunder of his heart and the hair on the back of his neck prickled. Anxiety slithered up his spine. He stiffened and his surroundings faded into a red haze as his survival instincts kicked to life. A growl vibrated up his throat and he whirled, ready to fight to the death.

But it was too late. He barely caught a glimpse of two shadows before he felt the stab in his neck. Pain gripped him, fierce and consuming. His muscles tightened. The ground seemed to shake.

And then everything went black.

19

SHE *WAS* AFRAID.

Meg finally admitted the truth to herself as she stood in the dressing room fifteen minutes later, trying to talk Honey Harwell into trying on dress number nine again since eight had failed like all the others. She saw the wistful look on the girl's face, the hidden longing, and she knew then that Honey wasn't turning down everything Meg showed her because she didn't like it.

No, she was turning down this particular dress because she liked it too much.

Because she loved it.

Just the way Meg was turning down Dillon. Running from him. Hiding.

Because she didn't want to take a chance, to fall in love, to end up brokenhearted and alone.

The truth crystallized as Honey ran her fingers over a row of buttons, her touch lingering a little too long before she made a face.

Yes, Dillon was right.

Meg was still the same person deep down inside, still nursing the same hurt, still scared.

Still alone.

And Dillon was still there.

Holding her. Helping her. Loving her.

He always had been.

And while she had no clue what tomorrow would bring—his salvation or an eternity as a vampire—suddenly it didn't matter. All that mattered was telling him that she loved him today.

Right now.

"It's yours," Meg told Honey as she set aside a stack of dresses.

"Excuse me?"

"I know you like this dress. You know you like this dress. So why don't you just admit it and end the misery for both of us?"

Honey popped a bubble with her gum, licking the sticky whiteness from her lips. "You're crazy, lady."

"And you're in denial. There's nothing wrong with wearing pretty things. Just like there's nothing wrong with wearing sweats and a lucky Cowboys T-shirt." When Honey's disdain turned to bewilderment, Meg rushed on, "Stop being afraid of yourself."

"I'm not afraid of anything."

"Yes, you are. Face it so you can get past it."

"What the hell do you know?"

"More than you can imagine." Her own hurt bubbled up deep inside her, but she didn't tamp it back down. Instead, she let it come, embracing it. Her eyes burned and the tears that had threatened her earlier slipped down her cheeks now.

Honey stiffened. "Geez lady, you don't have to get all emotional. I—I didn't mean to hurt your feelings."

Meg leveled a stare at the girl. "Do you really want to miss your one and only senior prom?"

"Maybe," Honey finally said after a long, contemplative moment. "I don't know."

"Then that means there's a part of you that wants to go." She wiped at her tears. "So take that dress and go. My treat."

An eager light glimmered in her eyes before fading into cold determination. "And look like the rest of my sisters? I have enough trouble getting my mom to notice me without blending in with the bunch."

"Is that what this is about, Honey Harwell?"

The familiar voice filled the room and Meg turned toward the curtained doorway to see Elise standing there.

"You're acting like a mule because you want my attention?"

"Hardly." Honey tossed the dress back at Meg. "The last thing I need is you hounding me."

It was the last thing she needed, and the one thing she desperately wanted.

Meg knew it and, thankfully, so did Elise.

The woman took one look at her daughter, grabbed the dress and thrust it at the young girl. "Put it on."

"I already hate it."

"Then we'll try on more until we find one that you don't hate. And we'll keep trying if we have to spend every single day here from now until prom." She smiled at her daughter. "That, or you could take this one and we could head over to the diner for a couple of diet sodas."

"Without Katy or Ellen or Marjorie or Sue?"

"Just us."

Excitement fueled the young girl's gaze as she motioned to dress number eight. "I'll take this one. And those gold shoes and the earrings I saw in the front window. And that necklace in the front case."

One problem solved. One to go.

Meg promised Elise to have everything boxed up and delivered tomorrow, then bid the mother and daughter goodnight. She was just about to lock the front door and see what she could do about tackling problem number two when she spied the black motorcycle still parked at the curb.

Hope flared, only to die a quick death when she walked outside. Fear slithered up her spine a split second before she heard the grumble of an engine. She turned toward her left in time to see a car pull out of the driveway behind the storefront next to hers. The Buick crept onto Main Street and headed North, away from her.

A strange sense of déjà vu swept over her and her mind rushed back to the parking lot at The Roundup. She saw the familiar blue paint and tinted windows.

Her hands and feet started to tingle and she knew then that something was desperately wrong.

Even before she heard Dillon's desperate voice.

Get help.

But she didn't have time. Despite the car's slow, steady pace, it was already near the main intersection of town. Once it turned onto the highway, it would pick up speed and be God knows where by the time she called Jake and Garret. While she had no doubt they would find him, they might not make it before...

The thought trailed off and fear rushed through her. Time sucked her back, paralyzing her for a brief moment.

The worst day of her life.

Not this time. Not if she could help it.

"Call Nikki Braxton," Meg told Terry as she rushed inside and snatched up her keys.

"What for?"

"Tell her Dillon's in trouble and he's headed for the interstate."

"Dillon? Dillon Cash? But he was just here."

"You saw him?"

"Yes." She seemed to think and the lightbulb that had clicked on in her head dulled. "I guess not. Where are you going?" Her voice followed Meg as she rushed back out the door.

"To help Dillon."

I'm coming. She sent the silent thought, climbed into her car and took off after the Buick.

MEG'S VOICE WHISPERED through his head, coaxing him from the smothering blackness that held him immobile.

They hit a bump and his body bounced, shaking him from the lethargy and jerking him back to reality. To the vinyl seat beneath him and the duct tape binding his wrists and ankles, and the voices coming from the front seat.

"Can't you drive any faster?" a woman's voice asked.

"You want me to get stopped?" The question was deep and inexplicably male. "There are state troopers up and down this road. The last thing we need to do is get pulled over with a body in our backseat."

"A vampire," the other voice corrected. "There's a big difference. You saw for yourself last night."

"Yeah, well I still ain't one-hundred-percent convinced, and I won't be until I'm holding one of those fangs in my hand. Until then, I'm taking this as if we were in the middle of a bona fide kidnapping. Any kidnapper worth his salt knows you don't speed when you got someone hog-tied in your backseat."

"So don't speed. But you can at least go the friggin' speed limit, can't you? That damned dart will wear off before we even get back to the motel at this rate."

But it was already wearing off, thanks to last night, Meg's sweet blood, and the voice that whispered through his head.

Hold on, she chanted. *Just...hold...on... There. I see them.*

Panic bolted through him. The last thing, the very last thing he wanted was for Meg to catch up to them while he was tied up and defenseless. She would wind up in the backseat next to him, at the mercy of whoever sat in the front seat.

He fought against the numbness and willed his hands to move. His fingers flexed and tightened. The tape snapped as easily as toilet paper.

"I hope you're right about this," the man muttered. "If we go to all this trouble and all we get is a couple hundred dollars, I'm going to be pissed."

"Just hush up. That grilled cheese sandwich with the Jesus image went for eight thousand dollars on eBay. You think a real vampire fang won't go for at least ten?"

"*If* it's real."

"It's real, already. You saw yourself last night at that honky tonk. Didn't I tell you?" the woman muttered. "I told you even before we headed down here. This guy's a vampire, all right. I knew it when I first saw the blog. I told you then, didn't I? The stuff he mentioned... Well, you just can't make shit like that up."

The words sank in and the truth dawned. Dillon knew then that he hadn't drawn the attention of vampire hunters, or even the Ancient One.

Not yet, that is.

No, he'd drawn a couple of crazies who wanted to auction off his fangs on eBay.

As ridiculous as it was, he couldn't deny the pain piercing the side of his neck where they'd shot him with another tranquilizer dart. To render him unconscious so they could take him to some seedy motel, tie him to a bed, rip out his fangs and make their fortune on the damned Internet.

Like hell.

He summoned his muscles to cooperate and eased up just enough to peer over the seat. His gaze dropped to the tranquilizer gun sitting on the cracked vinyl between them, right next to a pistol and a giant-size set of pliers.

Make that dangerous crazies.

"Holy shit," the driver muttered and swerved.

Dillon hit the seat and hissed as a wave of pain swamped him. He fought against the heat that needled him and focused on the voices.

"What's wrong?" The woman demanded.

"There's a car following us."

She shot a nervous glance over her shoulder. "Okay, fine, but don't put us in the nearest ditch. Just stay calm." She twisted back around and motioned to the right. "Pull over."

"But someone's on to us."

"And we need to take care of it. Now *pull over*."

The car started to slow and the pain eased enough for Dillon to focus.

A few bumps and they pulled off onto the shoulder.

Headlights blazed in the rearview mirror as Meg skidded to a stop behind them. She scrambled from behind the wheel.

Metal clicked as the woman fed bullets into the gun and cocked the trigger.

"Dillon!" Meg's frantic voice filled the air at the same time that Dillon reached over the seat and snatched the gun from the woman's hand.

"What the—" The question faded into a loud *crack* as the gun exploded.

The windshield shattered. The man and woman took one look at him and screamed. They scrambled from the front seat, rushed past Meg and headed for the surrounding trees.

Dillon had half a mind to go over him, but then he caught the distant rumble of motorcycles and he knew the cavalry was on its way. Jake and Garret would find the crazies soon enough and dissuade them from ever again pulling such a stunt.

Right now, Dillon had more important things to tend to.

"You're okay," Meg breathed as he climbed from the backseat and stared down at her. Her hands went to his face in a quick search-and-discovery mission before he could even answer.

He caught her hand and held it over his heart. "That depends on who's asking?" She gave him a puzzled look and he added, "If it's my friend, I'm fine. All parts present and accounted for. If it's my lover…" He let his voice trail off as he studied her face, searching for the truth, praying with all his heart that she didn't block him out this time.

He needed to know in the worst way.

As if she sensed his desperation, she stared up at him, meeting his gaze. Her eyes gleamed, shining with a love so fierce that it hit him like a sucker punch to the gut and he knew.

Deep in his heart, he *knew*.

"You were right," she said. "I was scared. I still am, but I'm willing to face that fear if it means being with you." She swallowed. "I love you, Dillon. I always have."

"Even when I couldn't kiss worth a crap?"

"Even then. I just didn't realize it." She read the doubt that still niggled at him and her hand touched his cheek. "You have to trust me just like I have to trust you."

He held her hand to his cheek. "I do. I love you."

"Even when I couldn't kiss worth a crap?"

When he hesitated, she gave him a playful punch. He caught her in his arms and drew her close. "Even then," he assured her. "I know the future seems uncertain, but everything will work out."

Her gaze met his. "We'll work it out."

He nodded. Whether it meant joining as man and wife and growing old together, or spending an eternity. Either way, they would be together. Now. Always.

"So which is it?" He eyed her. "Are you my lover or my friend?"

"Both," she murmured, and then she kissed him.

Epilogue

GARRET SAWYER STOOD off to the side of the deserted highway and eyed the man and woman standing catatonic in front of him. Thanks to their recent escape attempt, their clothes were ripped. Dirt caked their skin and leaves stuck to their hair. But they were here. Present and accounted for.

Which meant Garret and his buddies were safe.

For now.

Both the man and woman were repeat offenders recently released on bail. The man had a rap sheet longer than a first grader's list to Santa. The woman had been in and out of the system since she was twelve. Neither had ever committed anything more than a misdemeanor, except for an assault charge when the woman had gotten into a fight with her bigmouth neighbor and pelted her with a paintball gun.

They were small-time crooks who'd figured they'd get their hands on some righteous cash by selling real vamp fangs on the Internet.

A crazy scheme that wasn't the least bit funny.

He fought down the urge to grab them both, slam their heads together and knock some sense into them. But Garret Sawyer hadn't been around forever by losing his temper. He settled for something even more effective.

"Climb back into your car," he said, biting out the words, carefully, clearly, staring deep into the man's eyes. "Go back to wherever it is that you came from and forget all about us. You weren't here. We weren't here." He gave the guy one last sweeping glance. "And for Christ's sake, do something good for your fellow man."

When Jake arched an eyebrow at him, Garret shrugged. "As much trouble as these two have gotten into over the years, I figure they owe society big -ime."

He nailed the woman with a stare and repeated his spiel. A quick motion with his hands, and the couple scrambled into their damaged car. The engine roared, the Buick shifted into gear and just like that, everything went quiet.

"It's late," he murmured as he watched the headlights disappear in the distance. "We'd better get back to town." He turned back to his friends, but they'd already taken the hint and were bailing.

Dillon, still weak from the recent tranquilizer attempt, slid his arm around Meg and let her guide him toward her car. Nikki and Jake walked hand in hand to the custom-made chopper parked next to Garret's classic Harley.

Isolation slithered around him and yanked tight. A feeling he'd had more than once in the two hundred plus years that he'd been a vampire. Always standing on the outside and never really fitting in. It came with the territory.

And it had never really bothered him.

Until now.

You've smelled one too many exhaust fumes, buddy.

He stiffened and turned toward the Harley he'd spent the past month restoring. The bike's frame gleamed neon blue in the darkness, the chrome handlebars a nice contrast with the vivid color. A black-and-silver skull wrapped around the fuel tank. It was an original and the inspiration for one that Garret was working on right now for an investment banker out of Austin. A job he had to finish in the next two days, otherwise he lost the bonus he'd been promised.

And Garret didn't like to lose. He took his work seriously. Even more, he liked his work. It passed the time and that in itself was a godsend to a man who'd already been around one hundred and eighty years too long.

A temporary situation, he reminded himself.

While Dillon hadn't managed to lure out the Ancient One this time, the young vamp was onto something with his research and his blog. A little legwork from Jake and Garret to follow up on his leads, and they would be able to narrow things down considerably.

It was only a matter of time.

Hope fired inside of him, a feeling that was quickly snuffed out when he gripped the handlebars and started to straddle the leather seat.

A whisper of awareness drifted down his spine. He stiffened and his fingers clenched. His nerves shifted to red alert. Garret knew then that while Dillon had sensed his attackers rather than another bloodsucker, there truly was a fourth vampire in Skull Creek.

But it wasn't the Ancient One.

The realization should have eased the sudden pounding of his heart and the frantic tightening in his stomach.

It made it worse.

Because what lurked nearby was much more dangerous than a centuries old monster with annihilation on his mind.

His groin tightened and his nostrils flared. The truth hit him. *Her*.

The first woman he'd ever loved.

The only woman.

"Long time no see, Garret," her soft, familiar voice slid into his ears.

But it wasn't nearly long enough.

Because Viviana Darland hadn't just taken his heart way back when. She'd taken his soul, as well. And her presence in Skull Creek could only mean one thing.

They were in for trouble.

Big, *big* trouble.

* * * * *

*Look for LAST WOLF WATCHING
by Rhyannon Byrd—the exciting conclusion
in the BLOODRUNNERS miniseries
from Silhouette Nocturne.*

*Follow Michaela and Brody on their fierce journey
to find the truth and face the demons from the past,
as they reach the heart of the battle between
the Runners and the rogues.*

*Here is a sneak preview of book three,
LAST WOLF WATCHING.*

Michaela squinted, struggling to see through the impenetrable darkness. Everyone looked toward the Elders, but she knew Brody Carter still watched her. Michaela could feel the power of his gaze. Its heat. Its strength. And something that felt strangely like anger, though he had no reason to have any emotion toward her. Strangers from different worlds, brought together beneath the heavy silver moon on a night made for hell itself. That was their only connection.

The second she finished that thought, she knew it was a lie. But she couldn't deal with it now. Not tonight. Not when her whole world balanced on the edge of destruction.

Willing her backbone to keep her upright, Michaela Doucet focused on the towering blaze of a roaring bonfire that rose from the far side of the clearing, its orange flames burning with maniacal zeal against the inky black curtain of the night. Many of the Lycans had already shifted into their preternatural shapes, their fur-covered bodies standing like monstrous shadows at the edges of the forest as they waited with restless expectancy for her brother.

Her nineteen-year-old brother, Max, had been attacked by a rogue werewolf—a Lycan who preyed upon humans for food. Max had been bitten in the attack, which meant he was no longer human, but a breed of creature that existed between the two worlds of man and beast, much like the Bloodrunners themselves.

The Elders parted, and two hulking shapes emerged from the trees. In their wolf forms, the Lycans stood over seven feet tall, their legs bent at an odd angle as they stalked forward. They each held a thick chain that had been wound around their inside wrists, the twin lengths leading back into the shadows. The Lycans had taken no more than a few steps when they jerked on the chains, and her brother appeared.

Bound like an animal.

Biting at her trembling lower lip, she glanced left, then right, surprised to see that others had joined her. Now the Bloodrunners and their family and friends stood as a united force against the Silvercrest pack, which had yet to accept the fact that something sinister was eating away at its foundation—something that would rip down the protective walls that separated their world from the humans'. It occurred to Michaela that loyalties were being announced tonight—a separation made between those who would stand with the Runners in their fight against the rogues and those who blindly supported the pack's refusal to face reality. But all she could focus on was her brother. Max looked so hurt...so terrified.

"Leave him alone," she screamed, her soft-soled, black satin slip-ons struggling for purchase in the damp earth as she rushed toward Max, only to find herself lifted off the ground when a hard, heavily muscled arm clamped around her waist from behind, pulling her clear off her feet. "Damn it, let me down!" she snarled, unable to take her eyes off her brother as the golden-eyed Lycan kicked him.

Mindless with heartache and rage, Michaela clawed at the arm holding her, kicking her heels against whatever part of her captor's legs she could reach. "Stop it," a deep, husky voice grunted in her ear. "You're not helping him by losing it. I give you my word he'll survive the ceremony, but you have to keep it together."

"Nooooo!" she screamed, too hysterical to listen to reason. "You're monsters! All of you! Look what you've done to him! How dare you! *How dare you!*"

The arm tightened with a powerful flex of muscle, cinching her waist. Her breath sucked in on a sharp, wailing gasp.

"Shut up before you get both yourself and your brother killed. I will *not* let that happen. Do you understand me?" her captor growled, shaking her so hard that her teeth clicked together. "Do you understand me, Doucet?"

"Damn it," she cried, stricken as she watched one of the guards grab Max by his hair. Around them Lycans huffed and growled as they watched the spectacle, while others outright howled for the show to begin.

"That's enough!" the voice seethed in her ear. "They'll tear you apart before you even reach him, and I'll be damned if I'm going to stand here and watch you die."

Suddenly, through the haze of fear and agony and outrage in her mind, she finally recognized who'd caught her. *Brody.*

He held her in his arms, her body locked against his powerful form, her back to the burning heat of his chest. A low, keening sound of anguish tore through her, and her head dropped forward as hoarse sobs of pain ripped from her throat. "Let me go. I have to help him. *Please,*" she begged brokenly, knowing only that she needed to get to Max. "Let me go, Brody."

He muttered something against her hair, his breath warm against her scalp, and Michaela could have sworn it was a single word…. But she must have heard wrong. She was too upset. Too furious. Too terrified. She must be out of her mind.

Because it sounded as if he'd quietly snarled the word *never.*

REQUEST YOUR FREE BOOKS!

2 FREE NOVELS PLUS 2 FREE GIFTS!

HARLEQUIN®

Blaze™

Red-hot reads!

YES! Please send me 2 FREE Harlequin® Blaze™ novels and my 2 FREE gifts (gifts are worth about $10). After receiving them, if I don't wish to receive any more books, I can return the shipping statement marked "cancel". If I don't cancel, I will receive 6 brand-new novels every month and be billed just $4.24 per book in the U.S. or $4.71 per book in Canada, plus 25¢ shipping and handling per book and applicable taxes, if any*. That's a savings of 15% or more off the cover price! I understand that accepting the 2 free books and gifts places me under no obligation to buy anything. I can always return a shipment and cancel at any time. Even if I never buy another book, the two free books and gifts are mine to keep forever.

151 HDN ERVA 351 HDN ERUX

Name _____ (PLEASE PRINT)

Address _____ Apt. #

City _____ State/Prov. _____ Zip/Postal Code

Signature (if under 18, a parent or guardian must sign)

Mail to the Harlequin Reader Service:
IN U.S.A.: P.O. Box 1867, Buffalo, NY 14240-1867
IN CANADA: P.O. Box 609, Fort Erie, Ontario L2A 5X3

Not valid to current subscribers of Harlequin Blaze books.

Want to try two free books from another line?
Call 1-800-873-8635 or visit www.morefreebooks.com.

* Terms and prices subject to change without notice. N.Y. residents add applicable sales tax. Canadian residents will be charged applicable provincial taxes and GST. This offer is limited to one order per household. All orders subject to approval. Credit or debit balances in a customer's account(s) may be offset by any other outstanding balance owed by or to the customer. Please allow 4 to 6 weeks for delivery. Offer available while quantities last.

Your Privacy: Harlequin Books is committed to protecting your privacy. Our Privacy Policy is available online at www.eHarlequin.com or upon request from the Reader Service. From time to time we make our lists of customers available to reputable third parties who may have a product or service of interest to you. If you would prefer we not share your name and address, please check here. ☐

HB08

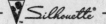

SPECIAL EDITION™

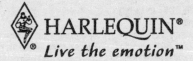

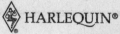

HARLEQUIN®

Blaze™

COMING NEXT MONTH

#393 INDULGE ME Isabel Sharpe
Forbidden Fantasies
Darcy Wolf has three wild fantasies she's going to fulfill before she leaves town.
But after seducing her hottie housepainter Tyler Houston, she might just have
to put Fantasy #2 and Fantasy #3 on hold!

#394 NIGHTCAP Kathleen O'Reilly
Those Sexy O'Sullivans, Bk. 3
Sean O'Sullivan—watch out! Three former college girlfriends have just hatched
a revenge plot on the world's most lovable womanizer. Cleo Hollings, in
particular, is anxious to get started on her make-life-difficult-for-Sean plan.
Only, she never guesses how difficult it will be for her when she starts sleeping
with the enemy.

#395 UP CLOSE AND PERSONAL Joanne Rock
Who's impersonating sizzling sensuality guru Jessica Winslow? Rocco Easton is
going undercover to find out. And he has to do it soon, because the identity thief
is getting braver, pretending to be Jessica everywhere—even in his bed!

#396 A SEXY TIME OF IT Cara Summers
Extreme
Bookstore owner Neely Rafferty can't believe it when she realizes that the time-
traveling she does in her dreams is actually real. And so, she soon discovers,
is the sexy time-cop who's come to stop her. Max Gale arrives in 2008 with a
job to do. And he'll do it, too—if Neely ever lets him out of her bed....

#397 FIRE IN THE BLOOD Kelley St. John
The Sexth Sense, Bk. 4
Chantalle Bedeau is being haunted by a particularly nasty ghost, and the only
person who can help her is medium Tristan Vicknair. Sure, she hasn't seen him
since their incredible one-night stand but what's the worst he can do—give her
the best sex of her life again?

#398 HAVE MERCY Jo Leigh
Do Not Disturb
Pet concierge Mercy Jones has seen it all working at the exclusive Hush Hotel
in Manhattan. But when sexy Will Desmond saunters in with his pooch she's
shocked by the fantasies he generates. This is one man who could unleash the
animal in Mercy!